The Shotgunner

The Shotgunner

Ray Hogan

THORNDIKE
CHIVERS

This Large Print book is published by Thorndike Press®, Waterville, Maine USA and by BBC Audiobooks, Ltd, Bath, England.

Published in 2003 in the U.S. by arrangement with Golden West Literary Agency.

Published in 2003 in the U.K. by arrangement with Golden West Literary Agency.

U.S. Hardcover 0-7862-5712-1 (Western)
U.K. Hardcover 0-7540-7357-2 (Chivers Large Print)
U.K. Softcover 0-7540-7358-0 (Camden Large Print)

The text of this Large Print edition is unabridged.
Other aspects of the book may vary from the original edition.

Set in 16 pt. Plantin by Myrna S. Raven.

Printed in the United States on permanent paper.

British Library Cataloguing-in-Publication Data available

Library of Congress Cataloging-in-Publication Data

Hogan, Ray, 1908–
    The shotgunner / by Ray Hogan.
        p. cm.
    ISBN 0-7862-5712-1 (lg. print : hc : alk. paper)
    1. Large type books.   I. Title.
PS3558.O3473S5 2003
    813'.54—dc21   2003054753

The Shotgunner

1

Tascosa. Raw, wild, lawless Tascosa.

But John Borrasco, the bounty hunter, was not interested in the town as such — only in one man he knew to be resting somewhere within the scatter of wind-scoured, sun-bleached shacks. He pulled up before Klinnman's Saloon and swung stiffly down from the saddle, a rangy, thick-shouldered, gray man with colorless eyes and a slash for a mouth. He paused, then, allowing his glance to rake the dusty street, deserted now in the mid-morning summer heat. Seeing nothing of interest, he turned back to the roughly hewed rail and looped the reins about it in a loose semblance of a knot.

"We got him this time, Jake boy," he murmured to the horse, patting him affectionately on the neck. The bay was a large, barrel-chested animal standing fully seventeen hands high, and alongside him Borrasco appeared smaller than average. "Reckon you can take your ease now for a spell."

Two of Klinnman's girls, pallid and

drawn-faced, came out onto the building's front gallery and stopped. Both surveyed the man with quick, appraising interest, saw no possibility of commerce in the weary Borrasco's appearance and strolled on. He watched their hip-slinging departure with a cynical eye. He shrugged and thought, Nothin' but kids, and up to their ears in trouble!

Just like this Dan Ruick he had trailed half across the country. Not much more than a boy, but with a reputation that befit a man twice his age. Said to have killed half a dozen men with that sawed-off shotgun of his — always in a fair fight, to be sure — but he had killed them just the same. They were all dead, there was no getting around that. Like the two brothers he had blasted into Kingdom Come, only there was a little different story to that. There had been no witnesses to that affair, no one to say it had been a matter of self-defense. He would stand trial for that little fracas. He would, that is, as soon as John Borrasco could lay hands on him and take him back.

Movement at the edge of town drew his vigilant attention at that moment. Two cowboys had halted at the end of the street. They conversed briefly, and, coming to some sort of agreement, each drew his pistol and set spurs to his horse. Both came riding breakneck down the strip of ankle-deep dust, yelling and firing their guns. Heads popped out of doors. Windows went up at once. A few of the braver residents came out into the open to see what it was all about. But the riders, their deviltry accomplished, had wheeled up before a saloon and stopped at the rack, laughing and shouting their greetings to acquaintances.

It was then that Borrasco saw Dan Ruick.

He had come from the shabby-fronted hotel and had leaned his tall, well-built frame against a porch roof-support, curious also as to the shooting. He was a wide-shouldered, narrow-hipped saddleman, and the weapon that had earned for him the title of The Shotgunner hung carelessly from the crook of his right arm.

"There he is, Jake," Borrasco said to the bay horse. "Now you just stand quiet. Soon's I have this jasper in the town's cooler for safekeepin', I'll be back and bed you down in a nice stall for the rest of the day."

Moving casually, he drifted around the big horse and into the passageway next to

Klinnman's. He moved unhurriedly until he was off the street, and then he quickened his pace as he traveled along the backs of the buildings that stood shoulder to shoulder at the street until, finally, he reached the hotel. He circled that building, coming around on its far side in such a manner as to bring himself out behind Dan Ruick. He hesitated before he reached the corner to check the heavy six-gun at his hip. He hoped he would not be forced to use it; he preferred to take Ruick back alive, since the reward for Ruick to stand trial was considerably more than that for Ruick to be buried. But in his business a man had to figure all eventualities. Satisfied with his weapon, he took half a dozen more soft steps, keeping hard by the building, and reached the corner. He stopped. Ruick was no longer on the porch.

Disappointment slogged through him. He had hoped this was the end of a long chase. Twice before Ruick had given him the slip; now it appeared he might do so again. Damn it! Why couldn't a man have a little luck once in a while? But he stood quietly and patiently, as was his nature, and watched the street. Perhaps Ruick had not seen him but had only sauntered off down the street, and would show up again in a moment or two.

"Right behind you, friend!"

The low, level-flowing voice of Dan Ruick was like icy water against his back. Borrasco froze, silently cursing himself for his own ineptness.

"Don't turn around! And keep your hands away from your sides!"

Borrasco heard the faint scuff of boot heels, then felt the sudden lessening of weight on his hip as his gun was jerked from the holster.

"You must have pushed that horse of yours the whole night," Ruick said then. "Figured you was at least a day behind me."

Borrasco turned slowly about to face the faintly smiling Ruick. He studied the younger man's square-cut, leather-brown face and smoky gray eyes. He shrugged. "Save us both a lot of time and trouble if you'd hand over that there scattergun and come along with me. No matter what, sooner or later I'll be takin' you in."

Ruick's lips curved downward into a scornful grin. "Go back and let them hang me?"

"Go back for a trial," Borrasco corrected.

"Wouldn't stand a dogie's chance in a wolf pack. Trial would be rigged from start to finish. Back there everybody's somebody else's relation. Step on one man's toe, you hurt a dozen others. No thanks, I'll just pass this hand."

"But you sure did kill them two brothers. That's a fact, ain't it?"

Ruick nodded slowly. "It was them or me — and two to my one. I had the right."

"Then there's no call to keep runnin' —"

"Like I said," Ruick cut in sharply, "this time I'll pass. I'll have none of your law. I know a stacked deck when I see it!"

In that succeeding fraction of time John Borrasco acted. With a downward sweep of his arm he knocked the barrel of Ruick's shotgun aside and lunged. Ruick, as quickly, stepped aside, his face a cold and expressionless mask. He wheeled, taking Borrasco's sledging fist on his neck. Anger flared in his eyes. The shotgun came around in a sun-flashed arc, the tall, well-thumbed hammers reared back for their forward plunge. John Borrasco saw the twin black holes of the muzzle, saw death ahead and waited.

The flaming anger seemed to melt from Dan Ruick. A dragging, tense moment went by. And then Ruick smiled in that faint, scornful way of his. "You tired of living? That's a mighty good start at finding the answer."

"Maybe you should have pulled them triggers!" the bounty man replied in a low, savage tone, barely controlled. " 'Cause you're goin' back with me, one way or another. I'll trail you till you drop. And I'll get you! No man ain't never got away from me yet, and I don't figure you to be the first one!"

"Maybe I will be," Ruick said easily. "Always a first time, they say. Now, supposing you just walk up ahead of me. We're going up to my room, using the hotel's back stairs. Nobody will see us that way."

Borrasco stiffened. "Your room?" he echoed, making no effort to start.

"My room," Ruick answered, "and either you walk up there on your own or I lay this shotgun across your head and carry you. Take your choice."

The bounty man shrugged and moved out. "What we goin' up to your room for?"

"You look like you could use a little sleep. Figured I'd turn my bed over to you, since I'll be riding on."

Borrasco said nothing. He did as he was directed, walking slightly ahead of Ruick up the rickety stair of the frame building and into the gloomy second-floor hallway. He paused there, and Ruick motioned with his gun to a door on the left — Number Six. They entered, and Ruick closed the panel behind them, twisting the key as he did so.

"On the bed," Ruick ordered brusquely, standing the shotgun against the wall.

John Borrasco saw, or thought he saw, his opportunity for escape in that moment. He lashed out at Ruick, putting everything he had in a straight, driving right. But Ruick, it seemed, was always a fraction ahead of him. The blow skated off the man's shoulder. Borrasco saw Ruick's balled fist suddenly coming at him, and there was a tremendous impact somewhere near the point of his chin. Lights popped brightly, and he felt himself go over backwards into darkness.

He came back to consciousness almost immediately, but not until Ruick had spread-eagled him on the bed, tying his wrists and ankles securely to the bedposts. As he watched the man complete his job, he thought of yelling for help, of trying to attract someone's attention. But his own strong pride immediately ruled that out. No, let Dan Ruick have his time; his own chance would come again. And again, if necessary.

Ruick, finished, looked down at him thoughtfully. "Reckon I'd better do this up right," he said. Glancing about the room, he took the dingy white cover off the washstand, ripped it down the center and made a gag, which he placed securely over Borrasco's mouth.

"Now you can catch up on all that sleep you been missing, chasing me. Don't think anybody will bother you until tomorrow morning."

Behind the near-suffocating mask, John Borrasco began to rage. For this to happen to him was unbelievable! But it had, and the man who was visiting such insult upon him was the very man he sought to capture! It was the most disgraceful thing in a lifetime of dealing with men. He watched Ruick collect his few belongings, stuff them into his saddlebags and turn to the door. There the tall rider paused, surveying him with a faint humor.

"See you in Mexico," he said, and let himself out into the hall.

Borrasco heard the lock click, a moment later the quiet closing of the outside door leading to the stairway. At once he began to struggle at the bonds pinning him down, but he succeeded only in drawing them tight. He lay back finally, breathless, sweat

15

pouring off him. Damn Ruick! Damn him to hell for this! He'd make him pay for it when he caught up next time. And next time he wouldn't be moving in with any thoughts of taking him alive. Next time it would be a different story.

The furious anger dwindled, then passed. A curious, disturbing thought crept into his mind. Out there in the yard — when they had first met and he had tried to break away from Dan Ruick and failed — Ruick could easily have killed him.

Why hadn't he?

2

Behind Dan Ruick lay the road to Tascosa
and seven years of other dusty, weary trails
leading to anywhere — and nowhere. The
endless miles across the booming Terri-
tories, the frontier states, through their val-
leys and over their plains; the length and
breadth of Texas, where still breathed the
crushed Confederacy; scorched Mexico with
its extremes of fabulous wealth and abject
poverty; Arizona, California, Nevada and
Virginia City with its seething turbulence.
But that was in the past; ahead lay the way
north: Montana, Wyoming, Canada — and
escape.

Now, he pulled to a halt at the head of
Saddlerock's twisted Front Street, the
thought of John Borrasco even then on his
trail turning him angry and impatient but
not dissuading him from his intention to
stop briefly. He stared moodily down the
twin row of buildings through expressionless, gray eyes. This was his town, his
home. And he hated it equally as much as
it hated him.

Seven years back he had ridden away

from it, carrying within his heart a depth of bitterness that had never washed from him. He had left behind his father and mother in the weed-grown graveyard beyond the church, a brother he near-worshiped and a girl — a girl who once had filled his dreams and given purpose to an otherwise miserable life but who, one spring day, had unexpectedly married that selfsame brother, Albert.

Dan sat quietly on the big roan horse, a tall, square-cornered, hard-planed man, broad hands folded over the horn of his old A-fork saddle, scuffed boots jammed deeply into the stirrups, and thought of John Borrasco. The bounty man would be on his trail again, possibly narrowing that half day and one night's lead Dan had manufactured by leaving him tied in that hotel room in Tascosa. That he had fooled Borrasco for long by dropping that remark about Mexico was unlikely — and so was his taking the road south out of town that day, after he had taken pity on the bounty man's weary bay and stabled him before he departed, even though he had made certain the hostler had seen him leave.

No one fooled John Borrasco much. He was a master at reading another man's mind, guessing his plans, figuring what he would most likely do when pressed. Just as he would realize Mexico was not in Dan Ruick's mind, that the Canadian border would be the logical place for him to seek safety. Borrasco was a good man, a smart one. And he was not the usual sort of blood-hungry bounty man you encountered, but more of a far-ranging lawman — feared and respected by all, a feeling Dan Ruick himself shared completely.

Often he had wished it were one of the others on his trail; not that he was hesitant to match guns with Borrasco, but simply because he knew it could end only one way — death for one or both of them. And Dan Ruick was no cold-blooded killer. He had never engaged in a gun-fight unless there had been no other way out; he had never shot down a man unless his hand had been forced. He did not want to be confronted by that choice with John Borrasco. Some time ago, he had decided the answer to that problem was to keep moving, keep out of Borrasco's reach, and in so doing that moment would never come.

He stirred, brushing the wide-brimmed hat to the back of his head. Trail dust lay heavily on his shoulders, graying the faded red of his shirt, discoloring the blue of his vest and cord pants. In reality, he had little cause to tarry in Saddlerock. He had no friends there, and he did not want to see the girl, Flora, but he would like to see Albert once again. A man never knew what lay beyond the next ridge. It was hard to forget all the things his older brother had done for him when they were kids — the beatings he took from the old man when he assumed the blame for something Dan had done, the fun they had had just roaming about when they were supposed to be working, the many things Albert had taught him. He reached idly for the sack of tobacco and fold of papers in an upper pocket and deftly spun up a thin cigarette. Weighing all things in his mind, he decided he would risk the time. But only a little of it, a couple of hours or so.

He lifted his gaze and let it probe slowly down Front Street. Saddlerock had changed little, if at all. It appeared just as worn, just as weather-thrashed as ever. At that moment it looked as though it had been forsaken and was no more than a ghost town, peopled only by dust devils, scurrying ground squirrels and the echoes of the past. But the old familiar names were still to be seen — Ward Lockhausen's saloon and gambling house, still the largest structure on the street, the Star Café right next door, then Fletcher's Bakery. The Longhorn was still the only hotel, and Tom Barr was still doing his hardware business behind the warped false front of his building.

There was Higinio Vaca's general merchandise store. Old Higinio hadn't been so bad, Dan recalled, allowing his eyes to settle momentarily on the store. He was the only one in the town, on the entire Silver Flats in fact, who had treated the Ruicks halfway decently — like maybe they were people instead of something to be stepped on and stamped out.

On the opposing side of Front Street, Dan noted that the Yake brothers were still around — Carl, the thick-shouldered blacksmith, and Ivan, who ran the feed and hay store. And next to them Martin Gonzales operated his livery stable. He wondered whether Martin still hated the *gringos* as much as ever. Martin had hated them with a passion because they had stolen the Mexican people's land, but, nevertheless, he had always been ready and willing to accept the *gringos'* silver as payment for his services.

The Kearney Code had been the cause of it, Martin had always said, referring to the American officer whose bloodless conquest of New Mexico in the late 1840's had led to his attempt to establish a clear and absolute title for the owners of the welter of land grants the king of Spain had parceled out to the *ricos* of the then Spanish province. Kearney had given the Spanish and Mexican people five years in which to register their property officially, at no cost to them. Many had, and thus still possessed their acreage without claim blemish. But a great number had not, either because of misunderstanding, not caring or simply because they had refused to accept the army man's authority and had elected not to bow to the dictates of the new government.

They were the ones who one day awakened to see the *gringos* moving in and settling upon their beloved land, taking over with legal papers enforced by lawmen. They were not the discontented ones, the unhappy ones, and their champion had been big and loud Martin Gonzales, who ranted by the hour on the subject, made elaborate plans for dispossessing the interlopers and never admitted it was a hopeless cause. Some of the families had listened, but the majority of the Spanish and Mexican people had come to accept their fate, and now merely shrugged in their stoic way when the subject was brought up.

Just for the hell of it, Dan decided, he would stop by the livery stable on his way out, after visiting with Albert, and have some fun with Martin, ask him how he was getting along with the *gringos*. And he would say hello to Higinio Vaca, too, maybe even buy some supplies for the trail. But all the rest — Lockhausen, the Yakes, Barr, Fletcher, the whole town, including the surrounding ranches — could go hang so far as he was concerned.

He spurred the roan lightly, and the horse started slowly down the dusty street. Dan pointed him toward the rail at Lockhausen's Warbonnet. He was dry, and a beer was the first order of things; after that he would eat a bite or else, if he wasn't hungry, he would ride on out to the ranch and see Albert first.

There were a few new names to be seen, he noticed, amending his initial impression. A Dr. Shaughnessy had moved into the place where a boot maker had once plied his craft. There was a new jail and marshal's office, and next to it stood another newcomer — The Dunaway Land Co., Nathan Dunaway, Prop. The Silver Flats country would be pretty tough going

23

for a land speculator, Dan decided.

He saw Flora at that exact moment. She came from the Longhorn Hotel and entered the deserted street, a small boy of four or five at her side. Her son and Albert's undoubtedly, for he looked exactly as Albert had looked as a youngster. Hat pulled low over his face, Dan watched them.

It was as though he had never been away seven years. She had been a dance hall girl, and she still had a faculty for making herself attractive. She had arched her full, dark brows, added a little color beneath her eyes and applied a dash of rouge to her lips and rice powder to her cheeks. She was wearing a yellow dress of some sort of glistening material, cut full in the skirt, tight around the waist and with a ruffled neckline just high enough to be acceptable but low enough to reveal the smooth contours of her breasts and shoulders.

She was beautiful, and the thought moved slowly through Dan's mind that, after all that time and a marriage to his own brother, she still had the power to move him deeply, to disturb him and turn him inwardly restless. But she was Albert's wife, and he had no right to such thoughts. He shook them off savagely.

He pulled up before the Warbonnet, keeping his face from her. He was glad she was in town. Now he and Albert could have their visit together, unmarred by her presence. The roan halted at the rail, and Dan Ruick sat quietly while Flora and the boy stepped from the boardwalk into the street's fine dust and crossed over. She was apparently heading for the ladies' millinery and dress-making shop, which was sandwiched tightly between Dr. Shaughnessy's office and a building that had once housed a saloon.

He waited until Flora and her son had entered the shop and then swung down from the roan. He looped the reins over the bar and unhooked the double-barreled shotgun from the strap that held it to the saddlehorn. It was a short, wicked-looking weapon, well-worn in stock, the metal parts gleaming brightly from use. He handled it much as a man might handle a six-gun, his strong hand wrapped around the pistolgrip-style stock, the comb of which had been flattened to fit snugly up under his forearm. In a land where men relied mostly upon revolvers, Dan Ruick was the exception who put his faith and trust in a double-barreled weapon.

Tucking the shotgun under his arm, he

stepped up onto the wide gallery of the saloon, aware suddenly that he was the target for several pairs of eyes. Ignoring them, he had started across the porch for the ornate batwing doors when half a dozen riders, entering the town from the far end, caught his attention. One of the horses carried a man's obviously dead body draped across its saddle.

Pausing, Dan watched the group ride up to the marshal's office directly across from the Warbonnet and dismount. A large, heavy-faced man with hard-surfaced eyes swung immediately down and went inside. People were gathering quickly, coming from the stores, the hotel and other saloons. The drum of excited conversation began to fill the street.

Dan stepped off the porch and sauntered toward the crowd, listening absently to the run of talk.

"Shot right through the heart . . ."

"Ambushed, so Fay says. Some jasper a-hidin' in the bresh. This side of the McCall place."

"Dunaway sure ain't goin' to like this! Nobody ain't goin' to kill one of his men and get by with it!"

". . . Nope, Fay said they couldn't catch whoever did it. They tried, but whoever it was just faded out, like a Injun."

Dan walked in closer for a better look at the dead body. The marshal, closely followed by the big, dark man and a well-dressed individual, came into the open. The lawman went straight to the horse and began to loosen the ropes that lashed the body to the saddle.

"Anybody call Doc Shaughnessy?" the marshal asked of the crowd in general. "Bein' coroner, he ought to be here."

"I'll get him, Marshal Wilde," a young boy volunteered, and trotted off.

The lawman went back to his task. Without looking up he called out "Fay? Where's Fay Grote?"

"Here." The man who had first dismounted answered and pushed through the gathering.

"You say you didn't get no look at the killer? Not even a quick one? You see his horse?"

Grote shook his head. "We didn't see nothin', Harvey. We was just settin' there when this bird, wherever he was, cut loose with a rifle. We tried to run him down, but he sure got hisself hid out quick."

The well-dressed man clucked. Swinging his glance over the crowd, he said, "Terrible, terrible thing. Just pure murder, nothing else. Marshal, you've got to get right on this. Find the man who did it and bring him in. Justice is one thing —"

Dan Ruick did not hear the rest. The lawman, in freeing the body from the saddle, had turned the waxlike, bloodless face toward the street.

The dead man was Albert Ruick.

3

At about the same moment Dan Ruick had been taking his first look at Saddlerock after a seven-year interlude, Marshal Harvey Wilde had been leaning back against the wall of his office and listening to Nathan Dunaway's smooth flow of precise words.

"Time is growing short. Necessary I complete these last transactions without further delay. We must bring Heggem and Sharp to terms. And then McCall and Brunk."

"Fair-sized chore," the lawman drawled.

"Perhaps," Dunaway replied. "There's one thing certain — I'm through with this velvet-glove approach. I am giving Grote orders to handle it any way he sees fit."

The marshal considered that statement for a time. He wagged his head doubtfully. "Might not be smart. You know how Fay is. Now, so far we been able to get the places you wanted without big trouble. You tell Fay to get rough and things could start kickin' right back in your face. Ain't you got enough land bought up for that friend of yours without takin' on Sharp's

29

and them others?"

Dunaway, who had been sitting at the lawman's scarred roll-top desk, got to his feet. A man of average height and weight, he had sandy brown hair, close-set, brown eyes and a thin line of pale color for a mouth. He wore expensive clothing, all imported from a tailoring house in St. Louis, and now he brushed at a smear of dust on the knife-creased trousers.

He said, "My plans are not completed until I have those four remaining ranches. That done, I will then own the entire northeastern corner of the territory, unbroken. Only then will I be in position to negotiate with my client."

"Must be a mighty big client," Wilde said. "What's he want with all that land? He plannin' to secede from the Territory and start one of his own?"

"What they plan to do is entirely —" Dunaway began, but the marshal's quick, slashing question cut him off.

"They? You mean it's some kind of a syndicate?"

Dunaway shook his head. "Forget it. You're being paid well to do the job I want done. That job does not include my furnishing you with a bill of particulars on my client. Let's keep things on that basis."

30

"Heard it was a syndicate," Wilde muttered, half aloud. "Reckon I was hearin' right."

"You just look after the law end of it," Dunaway snapped.

Harvey Wilde turned his ruddy face from the street to meet Dunaway's gaze. "Now, I been doin' just that, ain't I? But a man's got a right to know what's goin' on, that's all. Can't see as it makes a difference anyhow. One man or a syndicate, all the same to me."

Satisfied, Dunaway nodded. Then, "Where did you hear about it being a syndicate — or that it might be?"

The lawman shrugged. "Can't rightly recollect offhand. Over at the Warbonnet, I think"

"Was it Ward Lockhausen?"

Wilde pondered for a long minute, trying to recall whether it had been the saloonkeeper or someone else who had been talking at the time. Finally, he shook his head. "Danged if I can remember! Don't seem like it was Ward. But it sure could have been. I was standin' there —"

Dunaway broke in. "Regardless, if you hear it mentioned again, stop it right then and there. You tell them it's not true, that you know positively that it's not a fact. Understand?"

"Sure, sure," Wilde said, tired of the conversation. He swiveled his attention back to the street, his watery old eyes crawling along the store-fronts disinterestedly. He had made a mistake, he realized now, in throwing in with the land speculator. His badge, his office meant nothing any more; he belonged to Nathan Dunaway, a tool just like Fay Grote and Willie Dry and all the other fast guns who hired out to him. And it was too late to pull out. A man just didn't up and walk out on Dunaway, as two men, who had tried and now lay in unmarked graves, had discovered.

He guessed he shouldn't be questioning Dunaway and his methods anyway; so far, he had been out little because of his affiliation with the man. In reality, when you came right down to it, his position in Saddlerock was stronger and he actually commanded more respect from the townspeople than ever before, due to Dunaway's backing. It seemed that having the land buyer behind him was an asset. And all he had done to acquire that support was look the other way when Fay Grote and his riders had to get a mite rough with a rancher who had other ideas about selling out to Dunaway.

There had been no really serious incident; no one had been killed. Dunaway was smart there. He would get what he wanted, and he would get it short of murder. That is, such was the way of it up until the present moment. Sounded now like he was going to tear the bars down for Grote to deal with the four holdouts as he saw fit. Three of them were old-timers on the Silver Flats — Gordon Sharp and his Rockingchair outfit, Leo Brunk of the Lazy B and John Heggem and his Diamond H. Only George McCall and the C-Bar-C were comparative newcomers. None of them was taking to being pushed around. But Dunaway's patience had run out; that was certain.

Wilde suddenly stiffened to attention, his gaze coming to a full stop on a lone rider who had halted at the end of the street. He squared himself around, straining for a better look.

Dunaway, in the act of lifting a cigar to his lips, glanced sharply at him. "What's the matter?"

Wilde said, "It's him! Sure as blazes, it's him!"

Dunaway moved to the lawman's shoulder. "It's who?"

"Dan Ruick. The Shotgunner, they call him."

"Shotgunner?"

Harvey Wilde nodded. "Carries a sawed-off shotgun all the time, instead of a six-shooter. Faster'n most men with it. Real hardcase."

Dunaway regarded the rider with interest. "Quite a reputation, that it?"

Wilde said, "Just about everybody's heard of him. Wanted dodgers on him from hell to the moon. Think I got a new one a few months ago. Seems he shot up a couple of brothers somewhere."

Nathan Dunaway puffed thoughtfully on his cigar. "You planning to arrest him?"

Wilde took a full minute to reply. "No, sir! Not me! No reason for me to. I sure don't want him for nothin', and I'll leave it to the U.S. Marshals and bounty hunters to pick him up on them other charges. He ain't been seen around here for six or seven years."

"You mean he's from here — from Saddlerock?"

"Sure. Didn't you catch the name — Ruick? He's Bert's brother. Pulled out and left everything with Bert one day." The lawman wagged his head dolefully. "Sure hope he don't figure to hang around here for long."

"Bert Ruick's brother," Dunaway mused, watching the rider, slanting now for the Warbonnet at a leisurely pace.

"He's a real tough one. And trouble — big trouble. Every time he shows up some place, things start poppin'."

"Could be the very man I need."

"Need?" Wilde echoed, wheeling about. "What would you be needin' him for?"

"Simple. A man with his reputation likely could bring these holdout ranchers to quick terms. Reputation like he has does odd things to people, make them do things they might ordinarily balk at. You say you've got a wanted poster on him?"

Wilde turned to his desk. He rummaged through a stack of yellowed, dog-eared papers. Pulling one, he handed it to the land speculator. "Here's one."

Dunaway scanned it quickly. "Murder, all right. Two brothers. Ruick claimed self-defense, but there was no witness. And, with his record, he naturally had no chance with the law. Broke jail while waiting for trial."

Dunaway returned the poster, his light eyes vacant with thought. "This man is a godsend. Harvey, I want you to arrest Ruick. Use this dodger as your authority."

"Arrest him?" Wilde exclaimed in a

shocked voice. "Not me! He behaves himself while he's in my town, he's got the run of the place. I just plain don't want nothin' to do with tryin' to take him in for this murder charge. Leave that to somebody else."

"You arrest him," Dunaway repeated firmly. "If you need help, deputize Grote and Willie Dry. All the rest of the boys, too, if you want it that way. Lock him up. I'll take it from there."

"But why? I don't see —"

"Use your head, man! I need a Dan Ruick — The Shotgunner, as you call him. Need him long enough to bring Sharp and the other ranchers into line. A man like him working for me will make them want to talk and talk quick."

"But why arrest him?"

"Just outright hiring him might be hard to do. His kind don't always take to a job. But getting arrested for murder and then being paroled to me puts him under my thumb. When I'm done with him you can either turn him loose or send for a U.S. marshal, whichever you want to do."

Wilde wagged his head. "He ain't goin' to take kindly to no arrest. He don't like this town anyway."

"No? Why not?"

"A bunch of the citizens hung his pappy out at the edge of town a few years ago. He ain't likely to forget about that. Reckon I'd better wait until Fay and the boys come in. No use startin' a ruckus that might get somebody hurt bad."

"Won't have to wait long," Dunaway said, glancing out the window. "They're riding in now." He paused, his brow drawing into a frown. "Looks like there's been trouble."

"Trouble?" Harvey Wilde switched his attention to the oncoming horsemen. "By jeevies, that's a body they got draped over that saddle!!"

"I can see that," Dunaway murmured in a falling voice. "But whose body is it?"

"Looks like Bert Ruick!"

"His sorrel horse, all right."

The riders pulled up before the jail and halted. Fay Grote dismounted and came hurriedly through the doorway.

"Somebody potted Ruick," he announced in an angry, breathless way. "Put a rifle bullet through him from the brush. Now maybe you'll let me handle this my way!"

"Possibly," Dunaway replied coolly. "Where did it happen?"

"Near the McCall place."

Dunaway was only half listening. He was watching Dan Ruick, who had paused on the porch of the Warbonnet, turn and now drift slowly toward the assembling crowd.

Wilde started for the door. Dunaway said, "Hold it a minute, Harvey." The lawman stopped.

"You got any ideas who it might have been, Fay?"

Grote shrugged his heavy shoulders. "Had to be one of them ranchers. Or their hired hands. We hunted for a spell, but we didn't jump nobody."

"Good," Dunaway grunted. "Just wanted to be sure it wasn't one of our own hands." He faced Wilde. "Go on out there, Marshal, and do your duty. But forget what we were just talking about, about making that arrest, I mean. Matters are going to work out better in their own natural way."

4

At first, a lead-heavy, sickening grief slogged through Dan Ruick. Then blind, unreasoning anger took over. He shouldered his way roughly through the circle of onlookers toward the lawman, who was still tugging at the ropes. A horse, ridden by one of the men who had brought Albert's body in, barred his passage. He slapped the animal sharply on the rump, sending it shying off to one side.

"Hey!" the nearly dislodged rider snarled at him. "Who the hell you think you're shovin'?"

"Out of the way!" Dan said without looking up.

The cowboy, a red-headed husky with reckless, hard eyes, surged forward. He reached down and grabbed Dan by the collar. Instantly Dan spun. He seized the redhead's arm and jerked. The cowboy came piling out of the saddle and went sprawling full length in the dust. A shout went up from the crowd. Dan wheeled again, this time placing himself so he could watch both the cowboy and his companions. The redhead regained his feet and glared at Dan.

"Damn you!" he yelled, and rushed in fast.

Dan stopped him with the muzzle of his gun, jamming it hard into the cowboy's belly. With the back of his left hand he rapped him across the bridge of the nose. The redhead buckled first, then straightened up at the blow and staggered back. Silence had fallen over the crowd, and the marshal had paused in his chore.

Mouth blared open, sucking for breath, the cowboy stared at Dan. Wild anger flared in his eyes, and his mouth worked uncontrollably. "I'll kill you for that!" he managed after a few seconds. "I'll blow your guts —" His right hand lifted and settled slowly over the butt of the pistol at his hip.

Dan Ruick made no reply; he simply waited out the breathless heat-ridden moments. One of the riders suddenly spoke up.

"Pull in your horns, Willie, afore you get hurt. This time you're a-bitin' off more than you can chew."

"Nobody does that to me!" the redhead raged.

"Mind what I'm telling you," the other man warned. He was an older cowboy, his hair gray as winter dawn, his eyes flat and colorless. "I recognize this waddy. He's the one they call The Shotgunner. You make a move for that hogleg of your'n, and he'll blow you into pieces afore you can clear leather!"

A murmur rippled through the gathering. Willie glanced uncertainly at the speaker and back to Dan's cold face. From the porch of the jail Nathan Dunaway spoke.

"Forget it, Willie. No cause for a killing. One today on the Silver Flats is quite enough."

He came off the landing and moved up to Dan. "I gather from the marshal that you are Albert's brother. Sorry you had to arrive at such an unfortunate time."

Dan had swung back to the sorrel horse that was still carrying his brother's body. He brushed the lawman aside and, lifting the still form tenderly, laid it on the ground. Albert had changed; he looked old and very tired. He reminded Dan of his father.

"Somebody ought to tell his wife," a voice suggested from the depth of the crowd.

"She's right down the street. Saw her a few minutes ago."

"Get the parson. He's the one to tell her."

Dan stared down at Albert Ruick, and a hundred memories raced through him — memories of the good things they had seen and done together. Albert had been the only worth-while thing in his life, the one thing that had mattered. A surge of bitter hatred welled up within him.

"Who did it?"

He directed the question to Nathan Dunaway, who was standing before him. The land speculator glanced over his shoulder at the big man who had first dismounted. "Fay! Come over here."

Grote pushed his way to Dunaway's side. "Yeah?"

"Fay, this is Dan Ruick, Albert's brother. Fay's my foreman, Dan."

Dan did not extend his hand. His voice was low and cold as spring water when he placed his question. "Who killed him?"

Grote thrust his fists into his pockets, stared insolently at Dan and spat. "I knew that, I'd have settled with him myself. Albert was a friend of mine."

"But you're sure it was one of the holdout ranchers, that it?" Dunaway prompted.

"Had to be."

"Had to be — who?" Dan pressed softly.

"He means it had to be one of the ranchers who have been giving us trouble."

"Who — dammit!" Dan exploded suddenly, his patience gone.

"McCall or Gordon Sharp. Maybe John Heggem or Leo Brunk. Or one of their hired hands."

The stiffness in Dan Ruick's shoulders eased. He glanced again to the still figure lying in the dust. Now the one person in the world he cared for was gone — dead — murdered. Anger flared through him once more. Somebody was going to answer for this!

"You got an undertaker in this town?" he demanded of the crowd in general.

Dunaway said, "Of course. Couple of you men carry Bert over to Willoughby's."

"We had ought to wait for the doc," Harvey Wilde protested mildly. "Him bein' the coroner and such."

"I'll square it with Shaughnessy," Dunaway replied.

Dan remained rooted in the street, his eyes on the spot where Albert had lain. Around him the crowd began to thin, only a few of the curious remaining. He was thinking of his brother's death, of the need for finding his killer and evening the score

43

for Albert's sake — and he was thinking of John Borrasco drawing closer with each passing minute.

"How about a drink?" Dunaway suggested. "Expect you could use one."

Dan nodded. "Did somebody tell Flo — my brother's wife?"

"All been taken care of," Dunaway said briskly. "Let's get that drink. Got a little proposition I think you might be interested in."

"Proposition?"

"Like to persuade you to go to work for me. Sort of take your brother's place."

Dan glanced up. They were surrounded by a dozen or so men. Some he did not know, but there were those he remembered very well — Ward Lockhausen, Tom Barr, Ivan Yake, Fletcher. They had overheard Dunaway's offer, and their faces were stiff and sober. An odd streak of humor passed through Dan. Lifting his voice, deliberately baiting them, he asked, "Just what kind of a job?"

"Well, I'm buying up ranches in this part of the country."

"And you hire a crew to do it?"

"Don't know this country very well. That's the reason I hire men who do. That's why I gave your brother a job after

44

he sold out to me."

"Albert sold his ranch to you?"

"About a year ago. Decided to give up ranching. He and his family have been living here in town."

"Why don't you tell him all of the story?" Ward Lockhausen suggested drily. "That you hire gunmen to force men to sell out to you — at your price. And, if they won't, it means trouble."

Dunaway smiled patiently at the saloonman. "You've been listening to gossip again, Mr. Lockhausen. Certainly I make as good a deal as possible when I buy. That's only smart business. But as to the other — any man has recourse to the law if he feels he has been unfairly —"

Lockhausen laughed, a dry, scornful sound. "What law? You own that, too!"

"Now see here — wait a minute!" Harvey Wilde broke in, face red and angry. "You be a mite careful what you're sayin', Ward!"

"It's truth," Lockhausen replied evenly. "Any man with an ounce of guts will say it is."

Nathan Dunaway turned his back on Lockhausen. "Guess no man ever attempted to accomplish anything big without stepping on somebody's toes. Apparently I've done just that in this town. But it's no matter of consequence. You interested in the job?"

Dan allowed his gaze to stray off down the street. Where would John Borrasco be at that moment? A minute away — an hour — a day? If only he knew! A day, perhaps two, was all the time he would need — but dare he chance it? Should he risk a delay to satisfy his desire for bringing Albert's killer to justice or should he move on, knowing the bounty hunter was closing swiftly in? But surely he was at least one day or two ahead of Borrasco! He should calculate carefully, for it could mean his own life; Borrasco meant business this time, and there would be no escaping — alive, anyway.

He said slowly, "Guess not. Little short on time. Figure to take a day or so and run down the man who bushwhacked my brother. Then I'll be riding on."

"Working for me will tie right in with that," Dunaway pointed out hastily. "You'd have a better chance of finding the killer. You'll be dealing with the very people who did it."

Again Dan Ruick was silent. It did make sense, he had to admit. And it could save him some time — something that had suddenly become precious and dear to him. He lifted his glance to the land speculator.

"All right, so long as we understand each other."

"We do that," Dunaway declared, his shoulders relaxing in satisfaction. "I'll say it out right here before the boys — you work for me, but your big chore is to find the man who killed your brother. Something I personally want done, anyway. Can't have my men gunned down while they're out doing a job for me."

Dan only half heard him. His gaze was on Ward Lockhausen's face, stiff and disapproving. The saloonman seemed about to say something, his lips moving silently for a time. But he thought better of it apparently, and, whirling abruptly, he started for his establishment.

Dunaway, following the line of Dan's eyes, said, "Don't think friend Lockhausen approves of me. Or of you either since you've signed up with me."

The corners of Dan Ruick's mouth pulled down. He let his glance shift to the remaining crowd, seeing there the same heavy disapproval Lockhausen had evidenced. The saloonkeeper had been one of the lynch mob. And Ivan Yake, and Fletcher, along with several of the ranchers and probably a few in that very group now looking on.

"Means nothing to me," he said quietly. "Not what he or anybody else in this damn town thinks. Fact is, I owe them an old score. Maybe this will give me the chance to settle up."

Dunaway was somewhat startled by the bitterness in the tall rider's voice. His brows lifted sharply, but he recovered quickly. "Good, good. Now, how about that drink?"

Dan hesitated a moment. He had little time to waste over a drink, but he felt he needed one. "I'm ready. But it will have to be a short one. Got a few things to do and not much time to do them in."

Dunaway nodded as they turned toward the Warbonnet. Over his shoulder he called out, "Harvey, you and the boys meet me in the office in fifteen minutes."

The lawman said, "All right," adding, to the riders, "Reckon you heard him. Fifteen minutes."

Fay Grote separated himself from the others and swung in beside Dan and Nathan Dunaway, electing to accompany them. Dunaway shook his head.

"Stay with the boys, Fay. This is a sort of private conversation between Dan and myself."

Grote slowed and halted, his broad face darkening in embarrassment. One of the men snickered — Willie Dry, the redhead Dan had yanked from the saddle. Grote glared at the cowboy, wheeled angrily about and struck off down the street for another saloon.

Inwardly Dan Ruick sighed. Makes two I'll have to look out for, he thought. The redhead and now Grote.

And John Borrasco.

Shortly after midday, Borrasco, astride the barrel-chested bay, swung off the dusty road and pulled up beneath a lone tree that offered a small island of shadow beneath the blazing sun. He was not a large man and his weight was only average, but he knew the horse needed a few minutes' rest if they were to continue steadily on as they had been doing since daybreak.

"Get your breath, Jake, old boy," he said, loosening both cinches of the old Texas-style saddle. The soft and soothing words were strangely out of place, coming as they did from the thin, almost cruel lips of the man. But to him the bay meant everything — parents he had never known, wife he had never had, friends he had never made. Outside the fierce determination that bound him to his profession, the huge animal was his only other interest in a warped and solitary existence.

The saddle slack and easy, he moved to the bay's head and slipped off the bridle. "You know, Jake, I figure we're crowdin' that Shotgunner jasper mighty close. We already gained us a day. Maybe, come tomorrow, we'll pick up another. Now, you just take it quiet here in this shade."

He turned to the weather-worn saddlebags and took a towel out of the left one. Folding it thickly, he poured a quantity of water upon it from his canteen. Then he rubbed it gently over the horse's quivering lips and nostrils.

"Best I can do for you till we get to the next town. We get there, you're sure goin' to have yourself all the fresh water and grain you can hold. Way you been travelin', you got it comin'."

Borrasco paused and looked out over the long reaching flats. "Reckon it ain't far. Maybe be there, come dark."

The bay, through nuzzling the wet cloth, drifted off toward a spot of thin grass growing at the foot of the tree, but the bounty man did not move. He remained still, his gaze caught up in the distance. Unconsciously he tucked the cloth behind his gun belt and, drawing the makings from his shirt pocket, carefully and methodically built himself a cigarette. He struck the match with his thumbnail, inhaled deeply of the fired tobacco and tossed the sliver of burnt wood away. Movement in the steel-blue sky, high above the shimmering heat waves, caught his attention, and his hard-surfaced black eyes shifted. Buzzards. Near a dozen of them, sailing in a vast, gradually lowering circle. A steer down with a broken leg or something, he surmised, or perhaps a calf. Well off the main trail. He doubted if some human were involved.

But it made a man think a little. A man could get caught out there like that, hurt, and nobody'd ever know the difference. Only them danged winged scavengers. And maybe, if he was a man like John Borrasco, nobody'd ever miss him. The bounty hunter turned away, his thoughts making him uncomfortable. He shrugged, and the sunlight glistened off his tightly drawn face. What difference did it make how a man died? He had to die sometime.

5

Nathan Dunaway smiled with inward satisfaction as he watched the bystanders give way before Dan Ruick and himself. This was a fortunate day for him. He had long hoped to have a man at his side that all others would fear and respect. At first he had thought Fay Grote would be that person, but he had proved to be too heavy-handed, too obvious and crude. He had the brute strength, yes, and that utter lack of compunction so necessary when a job required ruthlessness. But his mien and manner provoked no respect — only a thinly veneered disgust and hate.

It was different with this man they called The Shotgunner. Ruick's quiet confidence, that aura of cool and efficient deadliness that clung to him like a threatening shroud, was powerful as a magic wand, brushing aside opposition, laying down a wide trail that would be easy to tread. Yes, it was a lucky day for Nathan Dunaway — trading ineffectual, useless Albert Ruick for his famous brother Dan. This could even work to better his chances with Flora.

He dropped his eyes in a sidewards glance to the wicked-looking, short-barreled weapon Dan Ruick carried so lightly in the crook of his arm. The gun was well worn, the shiny tops of the rabbit-ear hammers attesting to its considerable use. A man who depended upon such a weapon must be exceptionally expert with it, he decided. There could be many disadvantages — that it held but two shells, that its range would necessarily be of short distance, to name a couple. But apparently Dan Ruick had the answer to such drawbacks; else he would not be alive and walking down a street with the reputation he had acquired.

It would really be something to see him in action; something a man would remember and talk about when the subject of fast guns became the topic of conversation. And he would see him in action, soon. He was dead certain of that.

They crossed the porch of the Warbonnet shoulder to shoulder and pushed inside. The saloon was silent, the dozen or so patrons watching them cross the wide room and settle down at a table with no comment.

"What will it be, Dan, bourbon?"

Dan said shortly, "Suits me."

Dunaway called the order to the bartender. "Bottle of that good whisky, Charlie."

Ruick was not the best companion a man might choose, Dunaway reflected. Not very friendly, even a trifle on the surly side and entirely self-contained. And there was a tenseness about him, as though he wished to be moving, to be on his way, doing something. But that was all right. He wasn't hiring Dan Ruick for companionship but for his reputation. The bartender brought the bottle and two glasses. He placed the tumblers on the table, filled them and turned back to his counter. Conversation elsewhere in the Warbonnet had resumed its normal flow now the first curiosity had been satisfied.

"Fifty dollars a day, room and board?" Dunaway said after the first drink was down.

"Good enough," Dan replied.

"Have a house over on Lincoln street. Big two-story place with plenty of bunks. Got a good cook, too. Sleep and take your meals there with the rest of the boys."

Dan lifted his glance. "I'll look it over."

Dunaway decided it was the moment to show that he, after all, was running the show. He said, "Goes with the deal. You want to sleep and eat some place else, you'll have to pay for it out of your own pocket."

"Suits me," Dan said indifferently. "Always like to do my own choosing when it comes to where I eat and sleep."

"Of course," Dunaway agreed quickly. "You find a place you like better, let me know where it is. Maybe I can get you a better rate."

"Obliged," Dan said, "but don't trouble. You got anything else to say? If not, I'll be getting to work. Got to drop by and see Albert's widow before I do much more."

"Well," Dunaway said, stroking his chin, "I thought we might run over the job, the program I got in mind. Explain what it's all about."

"What's to explain? You're buying up land and you want it quick and at your own price. Anybody don't see it your way, you want their mind changed. That's it."

Dunaway smiled, his clean, even teeth showing whitely in the half gloom of the room. "Perfect. Couldn't have laid it out better myself. But you being from this town and some of the people being your friends, I thought you might feel —"

"Friends?" The word sounded like an oath. "Who said I had any friends around here? I hate the guts of every man jack in this country, and for a mighty good reason. That answer your question?"

"Completely," Dunaway said, making a mental note to ask Harvey Wilde the circumstances of old man Ruick's lynching. "One thing more. Fay Grote's been acting more or less as my foreman. You object to taking orders from him?"

"Let him keep the job. I sure don't want it, and I don't figure I'll be around here long enough for it to make a difference, anyway. I'm hunting the man who bushwhacked Albert. I find him, I'll be on my way."

Again Nathan Dunaway had the impression of haste, of Dan Ruick's desire to mount up and ride.

Ruick said then, "One thing you'd better tell that redheaded cowboy of yours is to keep his distance. I won't take much more of his foolishness."

"Willie Dry," Dunaway said, half aloud. "I'll settle him down. He's hot-blooded, and always spoiling for a fight. Fancies himself quite a scrapper. Don't worry, I'll straighten him out."

"Worry about him, not me," Dan said, rising. "Anything else on your mind?"

Dunaway shook his head. "Just wanted everything clear and understood between us. I think we've accomplished that. Drop by my place when you're through visiting Flora, and I'll introduce you around to the boys."

Dan nodded and swung about, the twin black muzzles of the shotgun pointing toward the door. Only then did Dunaway remember he had called a meeting at his office for the purpose of having Ruick meet his men. He started to call back the tall rider, but the wide shoulders of the man were already pushing aside the swinging doors. Dunaway hesitated, thinking twice.

Let him go, he decided. Most likely Ruick would ignore his summons if he did try to bring him back, and he did not care to have his authority flouted before the whole saloon.

A frown darkened his face. Dan Ruick had halted, his wedgelike shape silhouetted blackly in the doorway. Something was wrong; something outside in the street had checked him.

6

Dan pushed through the batwings of the Warbonnet and pulled up short as small, insistent flags of warning deep within turned him suddenly wary and alert.

He threw his hooded glance along the deserted street, then saw the half-crouched figure of Willie Dry poised, like a coiled rattlesnake, waiting. The cowboy's hat had been brushed to the back of his head, and a shock of his flaming hair swept out over his brow, giving him an almost boyish look.

Muted, careful sounds of movement from behind reached Dan's ears. He eased gently away from the doors until his back was against the solid wall of the building. He had not removed his eyes from Dry, but now he made a brief and thorough search along Front Street, seeking out the doorways, the passageways that lay between the structures, the shadows flattening out behind posts and the few trees where a man might hide. But Willie Dry was alone. The quarrel was of his own making.

"Been waitin' for you," the redhead

called, his voice cracking slightly under the strain of the moment. "We got us a little unfinished business to take care of."

A surge of anger flashed through Dan Ruick. Not so much at Willie Dry for his desire to face him — any man had the right to settle what he believed was an insult to his honor and dignity — but for the loss of time it involved. There were no minutes to spare, to waste, and a wave of impatience seized him.

"Forget it, kid," he snapped. "Be on your way. I got things to do."

Willie Dry straightened up, his face flushing deeply. "Maybe I ain't such a kid as you think," he said, unable to keep the tremor of rage from his voice.

"All right, you're no kid. Now get off the street and let me be."

Willie Dry shook his head stubbornly. "Ain't nobody slaps me around. Don't care how big a man he is."

"You asked for it and you got it. Take my advice and pull in your horns before you get hurt."

"I can take care of myself —"

"Maybe, but I doubt it. Move on. I've got no quarrel with you, and I'm in a hurry." Dan came slowly off the porch, talking as he did so. "Forget it. Go on inside and have a drink."

"Not till we got this settled."

"What settled? Whatever it is, best thing you can do is forget it. That way nobody gets hurt."

Somehow, sometime, during the few seconds the two had been talking, the shotgun hooked under Ruick's arm had slipped down until it was now in his right hand. The knuckle of Dan's trigger finger showed whitely as he put steady pressure on the bit of curved steel. The twin black holes were aimed directly at Willie Dry's belly. It needed only the lightning flash of Ruick's left hand, fanning the tall hammers of the gun, to send a charge of murderous lead into the cowboy.

Willie stared at the muzzle of the shotgun, fascinated. But his subconscious self recognized the terrible danger he faced if the conscious did not. He made no move to reach for the pistol at his hip.

"I figure you got things to do somewhere else," Dan said coolly, halting before the cowboy. "I know I have."

He reached forward with his left hand and lifted the redhead's gun from its holster. Without looking, he tossed it a dozen yards down the street, well beyond reach.

"Now, suppose you just turn around and

walk off. Pretty soon I'm going to get tired of looking at you."

Willie Dry came back to life then. He stared hard at Dan, then glanced hastily toward the Warbonnet to see who might be witnessing his humiliation. Then, with a throttled oath, he wheeled about and plunged down the passageway that lay between Yake's and the marshal's office.

Dan followed his blindly rushing shape until it was lost beyond a turn, and then he came slowly about. A few people had magically appeared along the street now that the danger from flying bullets was over. He scanned their faces until he found the one he sought — Fay Grote's. The man was leaning against the doorframe of the café next to Lockhausen's, his eyes squeezed down until they were half shut. Dan walked over to him.

"Better watch that boy of yours, Fay. I don't want any trouble with him, but, if he keeps pushing for it, he'll sure as hell get it."

"Not my boy," Grote said, sourly.

"Dunaway said you were ramrodding this outfit. That makes him your boy. You tell him to keep his shirt on around me."

Grote's attitude underwent a noticeable change. "All right, Ruick," he said in a more friendly tone. "I'll dress him down about it. He's too hotheaded for his own good, sure enough. I'll cool him down."

Dan gave the man a curt nod and swung away. He had little faith in Grote's ability to do anything at all with Dry, but the request had served its purpose; it had let Grote know he still considered him foreman and leader of Dunaway's men.

Ward Lockhausen had come out onto the porch of the Warbonnet, and, as he turned, Dan favored the saloonkeeper with a hard, insolent grin.

"Expected me to blow him in two, that it?"

Lockhausen nodded frankly. "I did."

"Sort of goes against your ideas about the Ruicks, that it? Well, next time maybe I'll accommodate you. Got to keep you believing we're just a bunch of trashy nogoods. You and the others around here been thinking that for years. No sense in changing now."

"Up to you," Lockhausen answered.

"Exactly. Now, mind telling me where I can find Albert's wife? Where they been living?"

Lockhausen said, "Apartment in the back of the hotel. Been there since Albert sold out to Dunaway."

Dan watched Lockhausen wheel and turn back into his saloon. He had not missed the slurring inference, the same old derogatory tone used whenever the name Ruick was mentioned. He had heard it all his life, up to the time he had left Saddlerock. It had not died away. It was like a brand; as though nothing more than the worst could be expected of the Ruicks.

Anger swept anew through Dan. What if Albert had sold out to Nathan Dunaway? What of it? Maybe he had good reason to sell, a perfectly sound and respectable cause. But, according to the way Lockhausen and the rest of the town viewed it, it had been wrong for him to do so. Well, he should have expected it. The hot words that would have scathed Ward Lockhausen melted from his lips. Forget it. It was all over with now, anyway. The Ruicks were finished in the Silver Flats country. He reached the step of the Longhorn Hotel and turned in. Forget it.

Albert and Flora's apartment was on the second floor, rear, the bald clerk behind the scarred desk informed him. Yes, Mrs. Ruick was in. She and the boy. Dan made his way up the dusty stair and down the narrow hallway to the last door. Outside he paused, taking stock of himself. All at once

63

he was unsure of his emotions; there had been a time when Flora had meant all things to him — now where would she stand?

He rapped lightly on the door and stepped back. After a moment there was a sound inside; the creak of bedsprings, the soft rustle of stiff cloth. Dry hinges creaked, and Flora Ruick, her eyes red from weeping, gazed up at him.

His impression of her on the street had been right, he saw; she had lost little of her beauty. The same fine, blonde hair, delicate as corn silk; the well-shaped mouth and pert, upturned nose. And now, those dark eyes, which had had such power to sway him, cut him loose in a fog of indecision and frustration. The hours they had once spent together came rushing back through his memory — and came to sudden, abrupt halt. This had been Albert's wife; she was his widow.

He watched her expression swiftly change at sight of him, saw her hand move to her lips, shutting off a cry of surprise. And he found himself watching with no particular feeling, only an objective detachment. She had changed little; it was he who had altered with the years. She was still the lovely woman he had known, but she no longer possessed the ability to enslave him that he had dreaded facing. A faint sigh of relief breathed through him.

"Dan? Dan Ruick?"

"Hello, Flora," he said, smiling.

She stared at him, unbelieving, for a full minute. Then, drawing him into the room, she flung herself upon him while a new storm of sobbing broke through her slim body.

Dan remained still, allowing her to expend her grief against his chest. He stroked her hair as a man might comfort an injured child, assuring her with quiet words that all was well, that everything would be all right and that she had nothing to fear in the future. As he stood there he let his glance take in the shabby rooms, the poor furnishings, the scanty belongings that were all his brother had to show for thirty years of living. Albert had been somewhat less than a good provider for his family. It was not difficult to determine that.

Flora's weeping ceased gradually. When it was over with, he took her slight shoulders in his hands and pushed her gently into one of the chairs. "Everything's going to be fine," he assured her once again.

She managed a wan smile. "I'm sorry to be such a baby, Dan. But I couldn't help it.

65

We don't have many of what you might call friends in this town, and seeing you standing there, coming right out of the blue, it seemed, was more than I could stand!"

"Bad time for you to be alone," he said. "Wasn't there somebody you could go to?"

She shook her head. "No one close. The parson and his wife, but it would only be sort of a duty to them. Nathan Dunaway, but I wouldn't go to him."

"I've already learned this town hasn't changed in the way it feels about the Ruicks," Dan said bitterly. "I reckon it never will."

She did not comment, signifying agreement by her silence. Then, "When did you ride in? I didn't know you were coming. Albert never told me."

"He didn't know, either. Was on my way north and decided to stop. Happened to get here about the same time they brought his body in."

Flora looked down at her hands, folded in her lap. "It's so hard to believe! I can't make myself understand what happened! This morning everything was all right. Albert walked out that door, just like he has every morning — and now he's dead! I can't believe he's really gone forever!"

"He is," Dan said softly, "and the sooner you make up your mind to that, the better. Where's the boy?"

"Out playing. He doesn't realize his daddy is dead." Her hands went suddenly to her eyes, and she began to weep again. "Oh, Dan! What can I do? What will I do?"

Dan surveyed the room again. "There's no money?"

"A dollar or two. No more than that."

Ruick was shocked. "What happened to the money Albert got for the ranch? I hear he sold out to Dunaway."

"There wasn't much, only a few hundred dollars, and that was a long time ago. When we got through paying off debts there wasn't much left."

"A few hundred dollars for the whole ranch?" Dan echoed. "It was worth at least a thousand."

Flora raised her swollen eyes to him. "Dunaway sets the prices, and that's what he pays. Albert was never much of a man to fight."

"I understand," Dan said slowly. "After that he went to work for him?"

"He was the only one in town who would give Albert a job. Nobody else would consider it."

"If Dunaway skinned Albert —" Dan murmured, thinking about the transaction, "I'll make him fork over —"

"Oh, there was nothing dishonest about it. Nathan is a smart business man. Too smart for the people around here. He just got the best of Albert, that's all, and Albert was never one to stand his ground in an argument. I guess that's why Dunaway gave Albert a job; he felt sorry for him — and for Danny and me. If he hadn't," she added, "I don't know what we would have done. Starved, I guess."

"Something would have turned up. Did I hear you call the boy Danny?"

Flora smiled. "Yes, after you. Albert would have it no other way. Nor would I."

"Not much of a name to saddle a youngster with," Dan said, pleased nevertheless. "Sure hope he turns out better than his uncle."

"I only hope he turns out half so well," Flora replied in a low voice. "One thing I've learned, Dan — success and money aren't everything. It's being happy with what you have and who you are. Took me a long time to find that out. Now it's too late for me."

She began to cry once more, broken and raggedly. But now there was something about her weeping that gave Dan the feeling her tears were not so much for her husband and his untimely death but for herself and the uncertain future lying before her. He walked to the small back window with its wavy, distorted pane and looked out upon the back yard of the hotel and the rolling plains that extended westward to the smoky Angostura hills in the far distance.

When she had regained control of herself, he said, "Important thing is what you do next. You have any people you and Danny can move in with?"

"Only a sister," she replied reluctantly. "She and her husband live on a farm in Ohio. We could go there. I don't know him, but I'm sure we'd be welcome."

She arose and moved to the window beside him. Laying her hand upon his shoulder, she turned him about until he faced her. "What are your plans, Dan? Could we — could we go with you? Maybe this isn't the place," she added, rushing the words, "but once I meant something to you, and so I *will* talk of it. There is no time for doing the nice things, for being ladylike.

"Seven years ago I let you go for your brother. I lived to regret that choice, but I

69

made the best of it and was a good wife to him. Were he alive today he would tell you it is so. But that part of my life ended today. It is done with, over. That mistake is behind me. Now I want to start living, having and enjoying the things I've missed. Do I make sense to you, Dan? What I am really trying to say is, can you find a place for me in your life?"

Dan looked down into her eyes, at the tear-stained, desperate oval of her face. He turned away, his glance again reaching through the window. A woman in a blue and white checkered bonnet was feeding chickens in a pen next to the hotel's stable, arcing grain in yellowish handfuls to the scrabbling fowls. But his mind was back in the past; he was searching through the dim recesses of his memory for an answer to her plea. Discovering nothing, he knew what his answer had to be.

"I'm sorry, Flora," he said, "I guess it's just too late. Once it could have worked, but it's all gone now. Anyway, settling down is not for me. Still too many places to see, too many hills to climb. I'll see that you and the boy never want for anything, that you get to your sister's in Ohio, but it will have to end there. I'm pulling out, just as soon as I've brought down Albert's murderer."

Flora made no reply. Her hands fell heavily away from his shoulders and she turned wearily back to the chair. "It was only a hope," she said forlornly. "The trailing, dangling end of a dream. I was wrong to hope it might come true."

"I'm sorry," he said, "real sorry, Flora."

"Don't be. It was my mistake. I made it. I cannot blame you for it."

He reached inside his shirt pocket and withdrew two gold eagles. Laying them on the table, he said, "You may need this. Use it for yourself and the boy. I'll take care of the coach fare to Ohio. And the money for expenses." He moved to the door. Pausing there, hand on the knob, he added, "The funeral — will it be this afternoon?"

She nodded woodenly. "At sundown."

"I'll come for you," he said, and stepped out into the gloomy hallway.

Fifty miles to the east, in the town called Twin Forks — barely more than a stable, a general merchandise store and several saloons and gambling houses — John Borrasco rode quietly up to the livery barn and dismounted. Since overnight business was a rare and privileged thing, the hostler took the proffered reins eagerly.

"Rub him down good," the bounty

hunter instructed. "Give him grain but not too much water. And see that the grain is clean, hear? None of the half dust stuff."

"Yes, sir," the hostler answered, adding, "you'll be stayin' the night?"

"Depends," Borasco said, turning away. "Might and might not." There was urgency, eagerness in his sharp features, as though he were looking for something or someone, and hoped the quest would end there. He took half a dozen steps and paused. "There a lawman in this burg?"

"Yep, town marshal. Office next to the store. You figure to stay the night, mister, I can put you up at my house. Ain't no hotel around here. Give you a good clean bed; bacon and eggs for breakfas', too."

"I'll remember that," Borrasco said. "Now, look after that horse."

He walked straight down the center of the street, little puffs of loose dust spurting out from beneath his boots at each footfall. The afternoon's slanting light struck harshly against his features, pointing up their narrowness, diminishing his too-small black eyes and giving his face the rapacious, sharp quality of a preying hawk. His head moved ceaselessly, swinging from side to side, missing nothing, seeing all things; his long-fingered right hand hovered slightly above the gun thonged to his hip, poised, a thunderbolt ready to strike. The solid, tangible embodiment of threat hovered about him.

He angled toward the door of the lawman's quarters. Before he could step up onto the narrow wooden platform fronting the ramshackle building, an old man with a straggling, tobacco-stained mustache came out to meet him.

"Name's Borrasco," the bounty hunter said, coming to a spread-legged halt. "You the marshal here?"

"You're a-lookin' at the badge," the old man said with little interest. "What's on your mind?"

"You see a man ride through here in the last day or so? Young fellow, husky. Carryin' a shotgun. Likely he'd be forkin' a roan horse."

The town marshal looked slyly at Borrasco. "How much you reckon the answer to that would be worth?"

"Damn little to you," Borrasco replied in a voice that brought the oldster up with a jerk.

"Saw him ride through early this mornin'. About daylight."

"Headin' west?"

"Yep, on the road to Saddlerock. He

some special friend of your'n?"

Borrasco ignored the question. "How far to this town of Saddlerock?"

"Nine, maybe ten hours. Dependin' on the hoss."

John Borrasco nodded contentedly. Good. That wasn't much of a ride. Give the bay an hour's rest and feed, and he could still do it in nine.

"I asked, he a friend of your'n, that young feller with the shotgun?"

Borrasco permitted himself a faint grin, as close as he ever came to a smile. "Mighty good friend. Been lookin' for him for quite a spell. Obliged, Marshal."

7

Dan Ruick came from the hotel's lobby out onto the gallery and halted. Time was slipping away, and there was much yet to be done. Every minute he spent doing something other than looking for Albert's killer lessened his chances that much — for John Borrasco, he knew, was granting him no recesses.

But where to begin?

He let his glance run along the street, checking the few people abroad in the afternoon's close heat. It could be any one of them, he thought, or it could be a man fifty miles distant on the Silver Flats. But there must be someone, somewhere, with an idea that would narrow down the field to some degree. To be sure, Grote and Dunaway were certain it was one of the four ranchers who were refusing to sell out — or one of their various hired hands; but that still would cover a good forty or fifty men. Besides, Dan Ruick was not so sure. Nathan Dunaway was anxious to close his deals with the holdout ranchers; therefore he would employ any means to bring them to terms, including persuading Dan Ruick that one of them was his brother's killer.

And it would be useless to try and obtain any information from Ward Lockhausen or any other merchant in the town. If they knew or had any inkling, they would not divulge it to him. Suddenly his thoughts came to a dead halt — Higinio Vaca! The old storekeeper would be a good bet — he would go talk with him.

He swung off the porch at once and headed for the roan, nodding briefly to one of Dunaway's riders, who was lounging against the front of Wilde's office. He mounted to the saddle and trotted for Vaca's place at the end of the street. But he was a minute late. Vaca was just climbing into a surrey as he reached the corner, two other men with him. Before Dan came in to a line with the store, they had driven off. He would have to wait until later to talk with the merchant.

He decided then he would ride out to the ranch and have a look around. He might possibly run into something that would give him an idea or a lead; in fact, although it was a remote hope, if the bushwhacker happened to be someone in the vicinity with a hate for all Ruicks, Dan might draw a shot from him. And that would solve the problem quickly. He put the roan to a lope and struck out in a direct trail across the Flats for the old family place.

An hour later he entered the yard, walking the roan slowly as the nostalgic grasp of memory laid its strong hold upon him. He let his eyes drift over the sagging, familiar structures, the few trees grown now to larger proportions, the corrals and pens. He looked at the old well, its crudely boarded sides rotting in the hot sun. No rope hung from its squealing pulley, and the wooden bucket lay on its side a dozen feet away, a splintered target for some passing rider's gun. How many buckets of water had he toted from that well into the house? Once he had thought he would never live long enough to count them.

He allowed the roan to wander deeper into the yard, to come to a halt beneath a thick, spreading cottonwood, where a broad patch of sweet grass had attracted his attention. Ground-reining the horse, he slid from the saddle and strolled to the house. It was forlorn, dilapidated, its front door sagging from one leather hinge, its windows like sightless, hollow eyes. The floor boards groaned underfoot as he entered.

Passing winds had piled sand into conical mounds beneath the window openings and in the doorways, and had laid a film of gray upon the ledges; yet the sand had hidden nothing — all was familiar, all once a part of him. A man may have disagreeable memories — many of them — of his boyhood home, but there are always the few good things — and they are what draw him back and what he remembers. And fused together they create a sort of sentimental reverence for what once had been.

He wandered aimlessly through the four small rooms, marveling at their diminutive size, and passed out onto the hardpack that lay between the house and the low-roofed barn. It, too, was a sagging, decaying hulk, showing evidence of age and weather outside and of having furnished shelter for more than one weary drifter on the inside. Unconsciously he glanced upwards to the cross-beamed, unfinished ceiling of the structure. A buggy whip, broken across the middle, hung limply over one of the timbers.

That, too, evoked its memory — of the day, when he had been 15 or 16, his father had come upon him practicing a quick draw with a rusty old cap and ball pistol he had found in an arroyo. His father, seizing the buggy whip, had begun to beat him unmercifully for lapsing into the "ways of the devil." Dan had taken the thrashing without a sound, until it had become apparent that his father intended to carry on until he begged for mercy. At that realization he had rebelled, wrenched the whip from his parent's hand, snapped it over his knee and hurled it into the depths of the barn, where it had lodged upon a rafter.

That was the beginning of the end for him at his father's place. From that moment on, no word ever passed between them. Six months later his father was dead, a year and Dan was gone, vowing never to return. Only he had, and now, as he stood within the shadowy coolness of the barn, he wished things might have been different, that he might have understood his father better — and his father, him. Perhaps, if his mother had lived . . .

A noise on the far side of the main house brought him around quickly. He moved to the doorway and glanced out. A woman astride a white mare was staring curiously at his roan, evidently wondering where its rider was. Even at that distance he could see she was a striking brunette, well-formed by nature, and that she sat her horse with the ease of a born rider. As he watched, she half turned and spoke to someone he could not see.

Ruick slipped to the rear of the barn, left by the back entrance and walked softly across the open yard to the corner of the main house, thus preventing the girl or her unseen companion from witnessing his approach. Moving along the wall of the building, he worked his way to the front and stepped into view.

The woman's horse started at his abrupt appearance, and her own eyes opened wide, showing her surprise. But she made no outcry. An older man, a stranger to Dan, was standing at the head of a bay, and a third visitor — gray-haired, sharp-faced, hunch-shouldered — was leaning forward in the seat of a dusty black buggy. That man Dan well knew — Gordon Sharp, owner of the vast Rockingchair spread that lay to the north. All three regarded him with cool, expressionless faces.

It was the man with the bay horse who finally broke the awkward silence. "I'm George McCall," he said in the unmistakable tones of a Southerner. "And my wife, Lilith. That's Mr. Gordon Sharp, owner of —"

"I know Mr. Sharp," Dan cut in, acknowledging the other introductions.

The old rancher twisted about in the seat for a better look. He squinted hard, craggy features and bristling, full moustache thrust against the bright sunlight.

"You that other Ruick boy?"

Dan said, the rancher's disparaging manner rubbing him raw, "I'm that other one."

"Ruick?" McCall repeated. "You haven't by chance come to take over your old family place?"

Sharp snorted. "Him? You can bet he ain't plannin' nothin' like that! He's the worst of the whole lot! He's the one that's the gunfighter. Goes around killin' and murderin' for pay. See that sawed-off shotgun he's carryin'? That's what he uses instead of a pistol. People call him The Shotgunner."

George McCall said nothing. His wife hesitated a moment and then urged the mare a few steps closer. She was considerably younger than her husband, Dan noticed, and her eyes were nearly black, they were such a deep blue. There was a happy scatter of freckles across the bridge of her small nose, and her full, nicely formed lips were set now in a serious line.

"Is that all true, Mr. Ruick? You are a gunman, for hire?"

Dan shrugged. "Ask your friend Sharp. He seems to know everything."

"I'm asking you," Lilith answered quietly.

"No, ma'am, I'm no hired gunslinger, if that's what you want to know."

"You're here, then, about your brother's death?"

Dan nodded. There was no point that he could see in explaining to them he was just passing through, that he had ridden into the matter by sheer accident.

"I'm sorry about your brother," Lilith said.

Ruick said, "Better feel sorry for the man who killed him. He's one of your crowd."

Gordon Sharp laughed, the sound high and cackling in the afternoon quiet. "Hear that? And him sayin' he's no gunfighter! He won't deny he's killed other men, I'll bet! And I'd guess there's a price on his head right this minute."

"Believe what you want," Dan replied. "You always did where the Ruicks were concerned. My father's dead because of you and people like you."

"His own fault!" the old rancher came back. "From the first day your tribe came into this country —"

"Let it pass, old man!" Dan's warning snapped across the yard like a metal-tipped bullwhip.

Sharp grunted and looked away. George McCall cleared his throat uneasily.

"Would you be interested in working for us?" Lilith asked in the following silence.

Sharp came around in startled surprise. McCall frowned. Making the most of the moment, Dan asked casually, "Just what kind of a job are you talking about, ma'am?"

"We need a good man; one, well, good with a gun. You've probably heard about Nathan Dunaway. There's only a few of us left to fight against him. He's hired gunmen to force his way, and the only chance we have is to stand up against him with the same kind."

"Just one man — just me against this Dunaway and all his gunslingers?" Dan asked, a faint thread of amusement coloring his voice. "Thank you for the compliment, Mrs. McCall. Maybe, if it was just you and your husband, I might be tempted to sign on because I don't know you folks. But for Sharp and the rest of the ranchers around here, I wouldn't kill a snake laying on their bedroll! Fact is, I hope Nathan Dunaway skins them out of every acre they own. Now, if you want to know why I feel that way, ask your friend, Mr. Sharp, someday."

Gordon Sharp swore softly under his breath. McCall looked to the ground, scuffling together a small mound of dirt with the toe of his boot. But Lilith smiled.

"Sorry to hear that, Mr. Ruick. We need help. This whole country does, against a man like Nathan Dunaway. I was hoping you could see your way clear to give it, but I understand your position. Certainly, vengeance is far more important."

"My brother was important," Dan corrected. "He was the only good thing I ever got out of this life. And now he's gone. That's a mighty big loss somebody's going to pay me for."

"I see," Lilith McCall said. "I suppose I can't really blame you."

"Don't waste no sympathy on him!" Gordon Sharp said sharply. "My guess is he's working for Dunaway right now!"

Dan faced the rancher. "That would be a good guess. But just to straighten you out, I'm working for him just long enough to run down the man who bushwhacked Albert. When that's done I'll pull out."

McCall exchanged glances with Sharp.

"Any idea who the killer might be?"

"Only that it's one of you ranchers. Or one of your hired hands. I'll find out soon enough." He slanted a sardonic look at Sharp. "Good way to get me off Dunaway's payroll and out of the country would be to tell me who it was."

"Go to blazes!" Sharp said promptly. "Only way you'll ever find out is to dig it up yourself. You won't get nobody to tell you."

"Just what I expected to hear from you," Dan replied coolly. "This justice of yours works one way, like I figured. Long as it's for your crowd, it's fine. Somebody like my old man, or my brother, it's a different story. Well, don't lose any sleep over it; I'll find out what I need to know."

He glanced at Lilith McCall. She was smiling at him.

"I'm sure you will, Mr. Ruick," she said, and wheeled the white mare about. "Good-by."

Dan touched the brim of his hat with a finger and watched them all pull out of the yard. Too bad the situation had to place him on the opposing side in this matter; he would like to help the McCalls.

And, if he had the time . . . Involuntarily

85

he glanced over his shoulder, toward his back trail. There was no one in sight, particularly John Borrasco. He had known that, but somehow he had to look to assure himself.

8

Returning to town at the end of the afternoon, Dan Ruick rode the roan into Martin Gonzales' livery barn and dismounted. Gonzales was not around, the hostler informed him, but was away for the day. Dan, after giving instructions as to the feeding and care of his horse, cut through the wagon yard at the rear of the establishment and crossed the vacant lots to Dunaway's house on Lincoln Street. It was not difficult to locate, being the only large two-storied residence on Saddlerock's one other street.

It was a frame building, not old, but already in need of paint. A good-sized barn stood at the rear, with a pole corral lying in the intervening ground. Three horses, saddled and bridled, waited in the enclosure, and, as Ruick strode up the wide board walk leading from the street, two men came out the front door and took up positions on either side. Dan recognized them as having been in the party that had brought in Albert's body. He halted at the edge of the porch.

"This Dunaway's house?"

"Reckon so," one of the riders answered. He was the one who had cautioned Willie Dry during his first encounter with Dan. "Name's Crandall. Friends call me Beaver."

"Glad to know you, Beaver," Dan said, and turned his attention to the other.

"He's Bill Humboldt," Crandall informed him.

"Proud to know you, Ruick," Humboldt said.

Neither man had offered his hand, nor had Dan. Both were typical hardcase drifters, men always on the move but willing to pause long enough if the money and job appealed to them and the pay was attractive enough. Tough men to buck in a scrap, Dan figured.

He said, "Dunaway around?"

Crandall shook his head. "Not yet. But he's comin'." He pointed with his chin over Dan's shoulder.

Ruick glanced back. The land buyer, flanked by Willie Dry and Fay Grote, was crossing the empty lots, headed for his house. Evidently he had noted Dan's arrival.

"Ruick," Crandall said then, "you don't owe me nothin', and I ain't no ways obliged to you, but I'll give you a smidgin of advice. Keep your eyes peeled around Willie. He's bad medicine, worse'n a tromped-on rattler, and he'll sure be lookin' for the chance to square things with you."

Dan said, "Thanks, Beaver. I'll do just that. I take it he's no friend of yours."

Crandall shrugged. "Well, I'll pull hardware with any man what walks, if I have to. But it'll be to his face, not his hindside."

"Thanks again," Dan said, grasping the meaning behind the words. Then, "Either of you tell me anything about my brother getting shot? Any ideas who it might be, I mean?"

Humboldt shook his head, and so did Beaver Crandall. "Fay told it pretty straight. Just about the way it was. We sure didn't see nobody."

Ruick nodded. "Appreciate your passing on any word you might get. I'm a little pressed for time, and I've got to get my hands on that jasper soon as possible."

Crandall grinned. "Understand what you mean, Ruick. Been in that spot once or twice myself."

Dunaway and the two riders reached the walk and turned toward the porch. He greeted Dan as he came up. "See you're getting acquainted. Meet all the boys?"

Before Dan could reply Crandall said, "Otey's upstairs, sleepin'."

"Wake him up," Dunaway ordered. "We'll have a little meeting."

They all went inside, going first into a somewhat narrow hallway. From its center a stairway mounted to the second floor. Crandall immediately started up the steps to arouse the sleeping member, Otis Kirby, while Dunaway and the others turned off into a large parlor, separated from the entrance foyer by a doorless archway. There was only a large, square table and a dozen or so straight-backed chairs in the room.

"Kitchen's in the back," Dunaway said to Dan, "and the mess hall is next to it. You bunk upstairs. Front rooms are my quarters, sort of combination living and office space, you might call it. Stable your horse in the back. Hostler will look after him."

As Ruick nodded his understanding, Crandall returned, with the heavy-eyed Kirby in tow, and they all gathered around the table.

Dunaway introduced the blond cowboy to Dan and said, "In case any of you hadn't heard, Dan Ruick has gone to work for me, with us. With his reputation I think he can be a big help."

Willie Dry snickered softly. Dunaway paused, and Dan covered the rider with a speculative glance. He thoughtfully rubbed the smooth stock of the shotgun, and for a moment he was tempted to rise and slap Willie Dry from his chair, but he let the urge slip by.

"And, while he's helping us, he'll be looking for the man who murdered his brother Bert," Dunaway continued. "I want you to give him all the help you can in that. If any of you have any ideas about who it was or can help Dan in any way, don't hold back. Tell him about it."

Dan had stopped polishing the wood of his gun. He glanced expectantly, hopefully, from the face of one man to the next. The faintest clue would give him somewhere to start; already a half day was gone, and he was exactly nowhere. But there were no suggestions, no advice forthcoming. He settled back, disappointed.

"Keep it in mind," Dunaway said then. "Keep your ears and eyes open when you're around town. And when you start moving in tomorrow."

"Tomorrow?" Fay Grote echoed.

Dunaway said, "Right. I think we've granted Sharp and the others all the time they deserve. Starting tomorrow, we will close those deals, one way or another."

"Good," the foreman grunted. "Gettin' a bit tired of this pussyfootin' around."

"All of you watch yourself tonight," Dunaway said then, rising. "Be ready to ride at sunup."

"Where we go first off?" Grote wanted to know.

"Sharp's. We get his place, we got control of the water south of him. That ought to make the McCalls easy to handle. A dam thrown up this time of the year would dry him out quick. I don't think we'll have to do it, but the idea will be a strong persuader for you. Get those two out of the picture and the others will fall easy."

Grote scratched at his stubbled chin. "Brunk and Heggem got big spreads. Might be smart to take them first."

"McCall's been doing a lot of talking. Trying to get the others not to sell out. I'll admit that two-bit place of theirs doesn't amount to much, but they've sort of worked themselves up to the leaders of the bunch. They and Gordon Sharp. That's why I want those two out of the way first."

Grote nodded his understanding. "All right," he said, "it'll be Sharp's Rockingchair and then McCall's C-Bar-C." He paused, letting his eyes sweep about the table. "You heard what Mr. Dunaway said. Be ready to hit the saddle at sunup. And keep your lips buttoned up tonight. We don't want this nosed around." He halted again, this time turning his heavy-jowled face to Dan. "You want to pick yourself a bunk now?"

Dan said, "Never mind. Think I'll do my sleeping at the hotel."

There was a long moment of silence. Willie Dry broke it with, "What's the trouble, company not good enough for you around here?"

Dan returned the redhead's insolent gaze. "Do your own figuring, kid. Fact is, I need some shut-eye, and I don't think I'd get it around here tonight."

Beaver Crandall laughed appreciatively. Dunaway said, "Now, let's have no quarreling between ourselves. Dan wants to stay at the hotel, that's his privilege."

"No hard feelings, far as I'm concerned," Dan said, and started for the door. But he knew Willie Dry did not share his sentiments. The redhead was still pushing for a fight, and come it would, sooner or later, regardless of how much he tried to avoid it. He reached the doorway and stepped out onto the porch, pausing to glance back at Dry, assessing the man's thoughts and intentions. The redhead had not stirred. Good. It looked to Dan as though things would at least get through the night.

"Oh, Dan!" Dunaway's voice reached after him. "Like a word with you."

Together they walked into the yard. Dunaway said, "I'm wondering perhaps if you and Flora, and the boy, of course, might have supper with me this evening. After the funeral. Like to express my condolences to the lady in that manner."

Dan said, "Well, I don't know. Be up to Flora." It came to him in that moment that his brother's wife and the land buyer seemed pretty well acquainted, more so than might be expected of an employer and his employee's wife. He recalled, then, Flora saying something about Nathan Dunaway earlier, but just what she had said had slipped his mind.

"I'll be taking her to the funeral," he said. "I'll say something to her then. I'm putting her and the boy on the stage for Ohio when things are done with."

"She will be leaving?" Dunaway asked, unable to mask his surprise.

"First coach out," Dan answered. "Nothing around here for her and the boy now. Best place for them will be with kinfolk."

"I see," Dunaway said in a thoughtful voice. "Well, see you at the funeral. You can tell me then about the supper."

A quarter of an hour later, Nathan Dunaway, carrying through a previous idea, drew Marshal Wilde into his office and, closed the door.

"Had a little talk with Ruick in the saloon. I got the impression he hates this town and the people, or most of them, anyway, with a hellfire passion. I suppose it has something to do with his father. You know the details?"

The lawman nodded. "Happened before I got here, howsomever. I only know what I been told."

"Let's have it," Dunaway said crisply. "Might be something in it that would come in handy in controlling Dan Ruick."

"Well, a bunch of the people around here lynched old Joe Ruick. He never was much good. Drunk most of the time after his wife died, which was shortly after they blew into the Silver Flats country from somewhere east. That was after the war."

"Why did they hang him?"

"Comin' to that. Used to be a family here, name of Morton, or maybe it was Martin. Anyway, they had a place out east of town. Nice people, everybody says, and they was well liked. They had a daughter, poor thing, that wasn't just right in the head. Ever once in a while she'd run off, and they'd all have to get out and track her down."

"Grown girl?"

"Reckon she was twenty-four, twenty-five at the time. Anyway, one spring mornin' she turned up gone again. All the people in town and some of the ranchers started in lookin' for her. They hunted most all day but didn't turn her up, and I guess her folks begin to get real worried about it. About dark several of the ranchers workin' the draws west of here found them."

"Them?" Dunaway echoed. "Who?"

"The girl and old Joe Ruick. When they rode up he was tryin' to put his old great-coat on her. She was yellin' and screamin' and fightin' him off — and didn't have a stitch of clothes on."

"Great God!" Dunaway murmured under his breath.

"Guess things happened pretty fast after that. They took them both back to town. Course the girl couldn't tell them nothin'. Ruick claimed he was just ridin' through that part of the Flats when he come across the girl, naked as a jay-bird. It was cold, and he tried to put his coat on her. That's when the posse come up.

"But nobody believed him. Somebody remembered seein' Ruick leave town about the time the girl was supposed to have wandered off, and old Joe, him bein' drunk as usual, made it all add up the way they was thinkin'. In no time a'tall Ruick was swingin' from a tree."

"What about Ruick's family?"

"There was only the two boys. They didn't know nothin' about it till somebody fetched them and told them their pa'd been hung. Guess it hit them plenty hard, just bein' told straight off their pa'd been lynched for mistreatin' a woman. I don't know if they believed it or not, and I reckon they was too young to do much about it."

"Pretty slim proof to hang a man on," Dunaway said thoughtfully. "I understand now how Dan Ruick feels."

"Actually weren't no proof a'tall," Wilde said. "And I heard people say the gal had a habit of yankin' off all her clothes whenever she got one of her spells. But Joe Ruick bein' who and what he was, and the head men of that lynch mob bein' who they are, the whole thing was hushed up and dropped right soon."

"No wonder they left Bert Ruick strictly alone. And want nothing to do with Dan. He's like a thorn in their conscience. You know, Marshal," Dunaway added with a broad smile, "this fellow we call The Shotgunner is going to be a lot more valuable to us than I figured. We've got to keep him around at any cost!"

9

Dan got himself a room at the Longhorn and went immediately to it. Stripping, he washed himself down from the china bowl, shaved and donned a clean shirt. This done, he returned to the lobby and sought out the clerk.

"When's the next eastbound stage?"

"Ten o'clock tomorrow morning," the man said, examining some scribbled notations.

Dan reached into an inner pocket. "Two tickets. For Mrs. Ruick and her boy."

The clerk stared at him, momentarily surprised. Then, "Where to east?"

"Make it St. Louis. She can handle it from there. How much?"

The man named the fare, and Dan paid him with gold coins. "One thing more," he added, turning to leave. "I won't be around in the morning. You be sure they get on. You let that stage pull out without them and you've got trouble with me. That clear?"

The clerk looked injured. "Of course."

Dan retraced his steps to the stairway

and passed down the hall to Flora's door. At his knock she opened it, her eyes lighting up at sight of his tall shape.

"Come in, Dan," she said, stepping aside.

Dan entered, looking beyond her to the small, still child sitting stiffly on the edge of the bed.

Flora closed the door and faced him. "Danny," she called to the youngster, "come shake hands with your Uncle Dan. He's the one you were named for. He just rode in to see us today."

The boy came forward shyly. He shook Dan's hand, all the while watching his face closely. His gaze finally settled on the shotgun hooked over the big man's arm.

Flora frowned, noting his interest. "Must you always carry that — that weapon?"

Dan shrugged. "No man rides this country unarmed."

Flora shuddered. "And what does it get them? It certainly is no guarantee they'll stay alive! All it means for them is an early grave — a shallow one in a dusty, dry graveyard."

"Not quite that bad," Dan said gently. "This is a hard world and a man has to make the best of it — and look out for himself and the people who mean something to him. Only way he can do that is to be ready for all comers."

"Don't you have a pistol like my papa has?" Danny suddenly asked.

Dan smiled down at the boy, the image of Albert. "Just a little one," he said, patting the derringer inside his shirt.

"Can't we talk of something else?" Flora broke in faintly. "Something besides guns?"

Dan said, "Sure. I've arranged passage for you on the stage to St. Louis. I figure you can buy tickets for the rest of the trip there. I forgot to find out from you the name of the town you'll be going to, anyway."

She said, "Danfield," adding, "I'll be glad to leave this place. It's never meant anything to me but worry and trouble and grief."

He nodded his understanding. "By the way, Dunaway wanted us to have supper with him this evening. Told me to ask you."

"No!" she answered immediately, and the vehemence of her reply startled him. "No, Dan, please don't ask me to do that. I couldn't stand it."

Dan looked at her closely. "Something between you and Dunaway?"

"Not as far as I am concerned. He has always tried to be — well, more than a friend. Came by to see me several times when Albert was out working. Once or twice he invited me over to his place when my husband was gone all night. I — I never trusted him, Dan. And I'm a little afraid of him. And now I just don't want to see him. Does it make any difference to you?"

"None. You don't feel like going, so we won't go. I'll tell Dunaway that, and it will end there. However, there's nothing to keep us from having a last meal together at the restaurant, is there?"

She shook her head, but the meaning of his words was not lost to her. "You won't be here in the morning, then?"

"Dunaway wants us to ride — and I've got to find Albert's killer quick. But don't worry — you'll have no trouble about the stage. Just be ready to leave by ten o'clock. The clerk will see that you and Danny get a seat."

He moved toward the door, giving the youngster a broad wink as he did so. He glanced through the window to the lowering sun.

"Be back for you in about an hour," he said, and left.

Not counting Dan, Flora and the boy, there were nine people at Albert Ruick's funeral.

The preacher, his wife and the undertaker; Nathan Dunaway, Beaver Crandall, Grote, Marshal Wilde, Bill Humboldt and the hostler from Martin Gonzales' livery stable. The last four served as pallbearers, carrying their slight burden with considerable difficulty over the uneven ground of the desolate little plot.

Dan watched them with half-shut eyes. Maybe this was the proper way to bury a man when he was dead, he thought, moving his gaze across the weedy patch with its collection of drunken headstones leaning and sagging at all angles, its sunken rectangles of lifeless earth, but it was not his idea of where he wanted to be placed. If he had any say about it when his time came, he would choose the open prairie; there a man would still be free, and the sun could shine down on him and the winds blow in from the hills, and it wouldn't be so lonely.

The four men halted beside the open pit and slowly lowered their charge to the freshly turned mound of earth. The minister began his service, and Flora fell to weeping again in soft, smothered sobs, finding comfort in Dan's arm encircling her frail shoulders.

When the grim proceedings were all done with and Flora and her small son were again inside their rooms, Dan Ruick stood alone in the darkness of his own quarters and silently cursed the town and people of Saddlerock with all the bitterness in his scarred soul.

Even in death there was no forgiveness in them, no compromise. It would have taken little for Ward Lockhausen and Barr and some of the others to make an appearance. But they chose to remain aloof, chose to remember the way of things in the years that were gone; the name of Ruick was to be a blight forever.

So be it, Dan thought, grinding his clenched fist into his open palm. Let them have their way! Through Nathan Dunaway I'll make them wish they'd never heard the name Ruick!

Provided John Borrasco was not too close on his trail, he amended, walking to the window where he could look down upon the street and those who moved on it.

10

Willie Dry eased quietly up to the corner of the old K of P Hall and watched Dan Ruick, Flora and her small son come out of the Longhorn Hotel. It was near full dark, and lamps in the shop windows along the street had been lighted against approaching night. Several people were abroad, strolling along the board walks, soaking up the evening coolness.

Willie heard the regular beat of heels come up behind him, and then the voice of Otis Kirby reach through the shadows.

"Saw your gray at Yake's. Lose a shoe or somethin'?"

"Yeah," Willie answered, not removing his eyes from Dan Ruick. The tall rider, with his brother's widow and boy, was just passing the front of Lockhausen's saloon. The widow in her black dress, bonnet and veil looked like a drifting bit of the night.

"Pretty cozy," Willie Dry murmured, "he sure moved right in on Bert's widow. Sure didn't lose no time. Reckon old Bert ain't hardly cold, and here's his brother squirin' his woman about."

"Seems natural enough to me," 'Kirby observed. "She's got no other kin in town. Anyhow, I reckon it's their business."

"Sure, sure," the redhead replied. " 'Ceptin', him bein' so high and mighty and such. Better'n anybody else around. And now there he is, big as a bullfrog, makin' a play for his own sister-in-law. Could be he ain't so much as some people think!"

Kirby laughed. "Well, Willie, he sure did convince you!" he drawled, and sauntered off toward the Warbonnet.

Dry felt the hot blood surge into his neck as a flush of embarrassment and shame overcame him. He would never live down that slapping around Ruick had handed him! He knew it, well as he knew his name. Every time he looked at another man he could see they were thinking about it, remembering it and getting a big laugh out of it.

"That song ain't over yet!" he yelled after Kirby's retreating figure. "I still got me a verse to sing!"

Kirby came to an abrupt, flat-footed stop. He wheeled about quickly and retraced his steps. "Now, see here, Willie, you ain't figurin' to tangle with that Ruick again, are you?"

Willie mistook the amazement in Kirby's voice for admiration. "Just like I said," he stated in a low, confidential whisper. "I aim to sing that last verse."

"Forget it," Kirby said then. "No sense you gettin' your head blowed off. Reckon there's no disgrace to gettin' licked by another man in a fight. Lord knows I've had my plow cleaned many a time! You forget it, Willie."

"Me — I don't forget nothin'!"

"You better, kid," Kirby advised, his tone carrying a full warning. "This ain't just some saddle tramp you're goin' up against!"

"The way I like it," Dry declared. "I get through nailin' Mr. Shotgunner's hide to a fence, folks around here'll set up and take notice when I walk by!"

The Ruicks had reached the front of the Star Café and were turning in.

"That's right," Dry muttered approvingly. "Man always gets a good meal 'fore his execution."

Otis Kirby, a worried frown knotting his brow, stepped closer to his friend. "Come on, Willie, let's go have us a drink. Forget about Ruick."

Dry shook his head. "Get along, Otey. Leave me be. I got me some big plans.

Now, I ain't sayin' I'll be usin' them to-night or even tomorrow. Things has got to be my way, my own pickin' and choosin'. But I sure aim to get things done."

"You're plumb loco," Kirby said in disgust. "You better forget the whole thing. Come on and have a drink with me. They got a new gal at the Warbonnet. Sings and dances real good."

"You go ahead. Maybe I'll come along a little bit later and you can buy me a celebratin' drink."

"Willie, dang it — you better forget —" Kirby began, but Dry, suddenly irritated, slashed through his words.

"Go on! Get out of here and let me be! I know what I'm doin'!"

Kirby gave the redhead a long look, shrugged and turned away. "All right, Willie. See you later — I hope."

Dry laughed, the sound pleasing to his own ears. He had kind of shocked old Otey, he reckoned. He, no, none of them didn't figure he'd have the sand to stand up against Dan Ruick. Well, they were in for a mighty big surprise! He withdrew the six-gun from its holster and with a thumb flipped open the loading gate. Twirling the cylinder, he located the empty chamber and inserted a sixth cartridge. Closing it with a snap, he again spun the mechanism, assuring himself of its action. Satisfied all was well, he slid it lightly back into the well-oiled leather.

A fine ribbon of fire was coursing through Willie in those moments — a thin, white-hot stream that bolstered his nerves and made him a man ten feet tall. This would be his night; he would show them, every blasted one of them, he was as good — no, better — than this Dan Ruick and his scattergun! Then they'd show him some respect and they'd be calling him Mister Dry, not kid or even Willie.

Hell, he wasn't no kid! He was over twenty-one. Just because he still looked like he was young was no sign he hadn't grown up and was just as much a man as Ruick and the others. He'd prove it!

He moved off slowly down the street, then, keeping to the opposite side of the street from the Star Café, and came to a stop at the south corner of Yake's place. From there he could look straight into the restaurant and keep a close watch on Dan Ruick.

"Eat good," he muttered. "You'll need a full belly where you're goin'."

11

Dan Ruick, looking across the small breadth of red and white checked tablecloth, smiled at his namesake. The boy was finishing the last of his apple pie, his young face seriously bent to the purpose. It was pleasant in the café — cool from a breeze sifting in from the Silver Flats, filled with the low murmur of other voices in friendly and companionable conversation.

This is what a man forever on the drift misses most, he thought; this is what the trails, no matter where they lead, can never offer — a quiet, peaceful meal, a wife, a son, friendly faces.

Many times he had realized and been aware of the good things he had missed, but never so poignantly as this evening. It brought back the innumerable nights he had ridden lonely and adrift across the limitless plains and curving mountains, his eyes on a solitary lamp in some home-steader's window, a warm, yellow beacon in a solitude of blackness. Inside those walls, behind those pale lights were people, happy and content, and there was laughing and joking — and life, however hard, was a good thing.

Those things he missed. But a man played the cards dealt him. Events and other men were the true fates who carved out a man's destiny, shaped his life for him. Men like John Borrasco, ever on a man's trail, at his back, pushing him onward. Had it been any other way would he have chosen a life such as Albert had? Would he have been satisfied to settle down, living in peace and comfort, raising a family for himself? It was a question he often asked himself — but never answered. And, anyway, it was too late. Some things a man never realizes until it is too late.

He shifted his glance to Flora's calm face. She was looking across the room, her eyes reaching though the narrow window of the café into the darkness beyond on the street. Overhead lamps spilled their soft light upon her, softening her features, instilling a smokiness in her eyes and bringing out the delicate blonde loveliness of her. Maybe, if it had been Flora and himself from the start, it might be different for him. As it was he had never met a woman who had taken her place in his heart and mind.

He shrugged away his thoughts; why

consider impossible things? He glanced again at Danny. The pie had disappeared, and the youngster was regarding him in that grave way of his. He winked and smiled.

To Flora he said, "A fine meal. Now, I expect you're tired and would like to turn in. Tomorrow will be a long day, and you both will need your rest."

Flora brought her attention back from the far flung night. "I'm all right," she murmured, but the weariness in her tone belied the words.

"Coach leaves at ten. Get to bed now and do your packing in the morning. You will have time."

"I — I wish it wasn't so soon, the leaving, I mean. Everything has happened so fast. This morning, we were just as we have been for years, living here in Saddlerock, eating, worrying about the debts, trying to figure something better for Danny. By the same time tomorrow we will be a long way off, going to a new home in Ohio. And we will never see Albert again. It's so final!"

"You both will be better off away from here," Dan said gently. "Forget this town and all the people in it. They aren't worth remembering."

"I'm not sure I can forget. With Albert here —"

Dan shook his head. "I'm not much on this religion, but I remember one thing my father said after my mother died; that she wasn't out there in the graveyard, only a part of her; that she was really right beside us every day and night, no matter where we went. It's the only thing he ever said to me I remember, I guess."

Flora didn't answer for a long minute. Then, "I think he must be right but it's hard not to be lonely."

"That will pass. Once you are back there with your sister, talking of old times, meeting new people and seeing new things, you will get used to it. And you won't have any money problems. I'll see to that. I have enough to get you back there and keep you for a while. And I'll send more."

A frown knitted her brow. "I can't let you do that, Dan. It's not right that you should have to support me. I can get a job of some kind, maybe."

"This will be money that belongs to you," Dan answered quietly. "I'll collect it from Dunaway and mail it to you."

Alarm sprang at once into her eyes. "No — you mustn't! It's dangerous to cross Dunaway. You can't fight him, Dan! Nobody can. Try and you will end up like Albert!"

Dan grinned. "Never you worry about me. I know the Dunaways. You find them everywhere, and I've been up against them before."

She stared at him wordlessly. Then, "All right, Dan," she said in a dispirited voice, "I know you will do what you will do. But please don't take chances for my sake. We'll make out," she added, rising.

"Probably," he said, getting to his feet also, "but what belongs to you is yours. I'll see that you get it."

She gave him a baffled, hopeless look and, with the boy at her side, moved for the doorway. Dan paused at the counter and paid the check while the owner of the establishment eyed the shotgun crooked over his arm with disfavor.

It was completely dark now. Stars were bright in the depthless black overhead, and the street was a patchwork of light blocks tossed outward by the lamps in the unshuttered windows of the buildings. Not more than a dozen people were to be seen, strolling absently along, but in the Warbonnet and the other saloons the night was well under way. They walked slowly to the porch of the hotel, and there he halted.

Flora turned to face him.

"I guess this is good-by, Dan."

He nodded. "Likely I won't make it back before you leave in the morning. Good luck, and take care of yourself and the boy." He laid his hand on the youngster's head. "You mind your ma now, boy. Do what she tells you."

Reaching into an inside pocket then, he pulled out a small purse. Handing this to Flora he said, "Your tickets to St. Louis are paid for. Here's enough to take you the rest of the way and then some."

She started to protest, but he brushed it roughly aside. "Got all I need. And, besides, I'll be having a payday from Dunaway pretty soon."

"Thank you, Dan," she murmured and then, going up on tiptoe, she kissed him on the cheek. "You will take care of yourself?"

They were standing in the center of a pool of light coming from the hotel's front window. He grinned at her concern. "Man stays alive in this country only by being careful," he said. "Don't forget to write me your address so I can mail —"

"Ruick!"

The voice came reaching through the night from the shadows on the opposite side of the street. Willie Dry's voice.

"Get away from me!" he commanded Flora in a low voice. "Take the boy and get inside the hotel. Hurry!"

Flora and the youngster moved swiftly out of the light and onto the hotel's porch. Dan waited until he heard the screen door close behind them. Then he came slowly about to face the man waiting for him.

"You want to talk to me," he drawled, "step out where I can see you."

The redhead's stocky figure came from the deep shadows near Yake's feed store. Halting, hat brushed to the back of his head, he faced Ruick. "Been waitin' for you, Mister Shotgunner."

Dan settled himself firmly on his feet, a faint sigh slipping through his compressed lips. This was the way of things; this was always the answer. And the Willie Drys, honing to try their luck, were everywhere, plentiful as the greedy Dunaways.

"I've got no quarrel with you, redhead," he said then in a low voice. "Leastwise, unless you had something to do with killing my brother."

"He got hisself killed, that's all I know about it," Dry said. "But you're wrong about one thing — we have got us a quarrel, a big one, and I aim to settle it right now."

The street had cleared magically. But the noise within the Warbonnet slammed on — the laughing, the playing piano, the shrill voices. Off near the end of the town the church choir could be heard practicing for the coming Sunday services, the fast, quick tempo of the hymn *Bringing in The Sheaves* beating faintly along the buildings.

"You're a fool, Willie. You trying to prove something?"

"Maybe. Maybe I aim to prove you ain't such a big man."

"You can sure try," Dan said softly.

He watched the cowboy's hand come slowly upward and pause above the pistol at his hip. His own shoulders came slightly forward. The shotgun hung, muzzle down, in his right hand. He was keenly alert, awaiting that first betraying move on Dry's part, the tip-off that he was drawing.

He saw it. The slightest drop of the cowboy's arm for his weapon. The shotgun came up in a fluid, blurred arc. The comb of the stock smacked flatly against his forearm. His left hand swept across the tops of the twin barrels, fanning one of the tall hammers. There was a thunderous explosion. Willie Dry yelled as the slugs tore through him. His pistol fired, the bullet erupting dust at his feet. He staggered forward, twisted half about and fell heavily.

Dan Ruick broke open the shotgun and replaced the spent shell. Men were pouring out of the buildings, coming from the passageways into which they had ducked at the first signs of trouble, shouting their questions as they gathered about Willie. He felt a light pressure on his arm and, still taut, pivoted sharply. It was Flora.

"Are you all right?"

He nodded. "Did the boy see this?"

She said, "No, I sent him to bed."

"Good. Now go there yourself. This may not be over yet, and the street will be no place for you."

She turned obediently away and went inside the hotel. The crowd around the fallen Dry had increased, those who had witnessed the affair giving their versions of what had taken place. Willie had provoked the fight. Dan Ruick was not to be blamed.

"Course not," Ward Lockhausen's sarcastic voice answered. "Gunslingers like Ruick are never to blame for their killings. Somebody else always starts it, only they can't cope with what they've begun and end up dead. That's what makes a gunslinger what he is."

"But Ruick tried to talk him out of it!" one of the men in the crowd protested.

"Heard him with my own ears."

"I don't doubt that," Lockhausen replied. "But maybe it's a good thing anyway. Maybe that's the answer to our problem — getting rid of Dunaway and his bunch. Get them started fighting among themselves and kill each other off. Could be that's the solution for this country."

12

Get them fighting *among themselves and kill each other off!*

Dan Ruick slowly turned away from the crowd with the words of Ward Lockhausen revolving in his mind. If he had needed proof of the hatred Saddlerock felt for the land buyer and his crew, he had it now in those ten bitter words. It disturbed him, filled him with a strange sense of guilt, knowing he had teamed up with Dunaway and his bunch. Ordinarily, he would have chosen the opposing side with which to cast his lot. Dunaway's kind always angered him, and to find himself suddenly associated with such galled him deeply.

But the situation was entirely different in this case, he assured himself. Saddlerock and the people who were part of it were no friends of his; they deserved whatever they received at the hands of Nathan Dunaway, and he hoped it would be the worst. For himself, he was involved only to the extent that he was hunting his brother's killer. Once that task was completed Nathan Dunaway could take over the entire Territory, so far as he was concerned.

He drifted off down the street, past the Warbonnet, past the café where he had enjoyed the evening meal with Flora and young Danny. The encounter with Willie Dry had left him restless, and he did not want to return to his room but wanted to walk in the cool night and let the piled-up tension drain from his long body.

From the tail of his eye he caught the attention being given him by several townspeople along the way — cold, speculative, with a thinly veiled hostility underlying their covert glances. But he saw no actual danger lurking in the shadows for himself; it appeared Willie Dry would be mourned by few, if any, and avenged by no one at all.

He reached the corner of Higinio Vaca's store and pulled to a stop. For a time he let his gaze rest on the familiar front. He had planned to drop by the Mexican's place before he left, but with things moving so fast and the ever present thought of John Borrasco, the bounty hunter, lying in the back of his mind, he decided this might be his best and only opportunity. Abruptly he swung on his heel and crossed the gallery running the entire length of the building.

He pulled back the dust-blocked screen

door and stepped inside. The two hanging lamps had been lit, and the small, congested square of assorted merchandise was half in deep shadow, half in soft light. The store appeared empty, but at the slam of the screen Vaca parted the heavy curtains at the rear and shuffled into view. Vaca had aged considerably since Dan had last seen him, but then, to Dan, he had always been old. Thin, stooped, a small brown moon of a face. He halted behind the scarred counter and placed both hands, palms down, upon its surface.

"Señor?" he asked in the soft, polite way of the Spanish tongue.

Dan grinned at him. Vaca had not recognized him, but it could be due to the poor light.

"It's been a long time, *amigo,*" he replied, moving up to the counter, "but not that long."

"Years do not always make their changes, Dan Ruick," Vaca answered, his tone still stiffly polite. "It seems that is so now. In what way can I serve you?"

Dan's proffered hand lowered slowly to his side. A rush of anger flooded through him, and the old feeling of frustration, of being an outcast, unwanted, unwelcome, lifted again. He had hoped to find a friend in the storekeeper; he had hoped in vain.

"Forget it," he said brusquely. "Just passing through and figured to say hello. Just forget I dropped in."

Vaca's seamy face lifted. "Passing through? You do not plan to stay? If that is true, then the word that you are working for Nathan Dunaway is false."

"I'm working for him, for a spell. What difference does that make?"

"You have a saying among your people," Vaca replied with a shrug, "that birds of the same feather fly together. It is truth."

"Maybe, but just to keep it straight I'm working for Dunaway just long enough to find out who killed Albert."

"Ah, yes, poor Albert," Vaca murmured.

Behind him the curtains parted again, and the swarthy face of Martin Gonzales appeared. He moved into the room, deceptively quiet for so bulky a man, his beady eyes glittering like black raindrops.

"*Que pasa?*" he asked, sliding around to the end of the counter, close to Dan.

"It is nothing," Vaca replied. "Do you not recognize Dan Ruick?"

Dan nodded to the stable owner. It was impossible to miss the man's antagonistic manner. "*Como esta, Martin?*" he said.

Gonzales placed his hands on his hips

and stared at Dan insolently. "The bad dogs always come home," he said, and added, *"Cabrone gringo salado!"*

Anger crystallized in Dan Ruick. He took one, quick step to the right. In a lightning swing he backhanded the Mexican squarely across the mouth. The impact of the blow cracked like a shot, and Gonzales staggered back, an oath ripping from his bruised lips. His hand dropped to the pistol at his hip and then fell away as he looked into the twin barrel openings of Dan's shotgun.

"One thing more that's sure not changed is the size of your mouth," Dan observed sourly. "It always was too big, Martin."

"Why do you come back" Gonzales demanded, wiping at the blood trickling down his chin. "Is there not enough trouble in this country without you?"

"Something you'll get plenty more of," Dan replied, "if you don't keep out of my way. I wanted to be your friend once, even now, but you won't have it. So we'll let it ride as a mutual feeling. But stay clear of me, Martin."

"You say you would be a friend, yet you hire out to Nathan Dunaway?" Higinio Vaca broke in. "The two things are not *simpatico*. You cannot be both."

"Dunaway is just another man with money to pay for a job. Anyway, what's wrong with him?"

"A bad one! An evil one! One who kills and steals and lives on to do it again and again."

"Steals?"

"The land!" Martin Gonzales cried. "The worst of all thieves! He steals a man's home, his birthright — his land!"

Dan laughed harshly. Gonzales was still on the same old tack. "Seems I've heard that bellyache from you before. Nobody's fault but your own, and your people's, that you lost your land. If you all hadn't been so bull-headed and registered your grants like you were told to do, you wouldn't be losing your property."

Fury blazed in Gonzales' black eyes. He took a half step forward but froze as Dan's gun lifted slightly.

"It is not the same," Vaca said sadly. "That we could understand and come to accept. It was government business, and our people were wrong. Now it is another matter. This Dunaway is not the government."

"The devil himself!" Gonzales breathed.

Dan shrugged. "Like I said, I don't give a damn about him. Let him grab off all the land he wants. Fact is, I'll enjoy watching him root out Sharp and Heggem and all the rest of that bunch who always figured they were so high and mighty and better than anybody else."

"Hate is a terrible thing, Dan Ruick," Vaca murmured.

"And why shouldn't I hate them? All of them treated me and my people like we were dirt. I wouldn't turn a hand to help them! What they get from Dunaway, they deserve!"

"Then why do you come to my place? If you are their enemy, then also you are the enemy of my people and me."

"One reason. I know few things happen around here that you don't know about. I want to know who killed my brother."

Vaca shrugged his thin shoulders. "Hate and fear seal the lips of men. No longer am I the friend of all. I do not know who killed your brother. All I know is that the man who rides for Nathan Dunaway must always face the ambusher's bullet."

Dan swiveled his attention to Gonzales. "How about you? You any idea who it was?"

The stableman shook his head. "Who knows? Sharp — McCall — Brunk, maybe one of my own people. Perhaps it was I.

Like Vaca said, the ambush bullet is not careful of its victim."

"Meaning?"

"Perhaps the bullet was not meant for Albert but for another."

Higinio Vaca said, "It was truly meant for Nathan Dunaway, only it struck a man who worked for him. All the bullets that have been fired were, in reality, meant for him as a protest against that which he does. It is only that those who stand before him receive them and thus die."

Dan laughed. "You don't make much sense, old man. Question I want answered, and I don't have much time left to do it in, is who killed my brother. Who fired the shot?"

Vaca sighed. "If I could tell you, Dan Ruick, I would do so. For then you would go away and leave us to our trouble. In truth, I do not know."

"Then I will stay with Dunaway until I find him," Dan said. "If you and your people are hurt in the doing, I am sorry."

"All people will be hurt before this is done with," Vaca replied, and turned away sadly. "*Adios*, Dan Ruick. *Vaya con Dios*, and may His forgiveness come to you."

"*Adios*," Dan said, and swung his glance to Martin Gonzales. He studied the man's features for a moment, issuing a warning with his eyes and then wheeled to the door. *"Hasta luego,"* he said then, and stepped out onto the porch.

Crossing the pine planking, he entered the street. He halted suddenly, freezing in the black shadow of the building. A lone horseman was entering the dusty ribbon, coming in from the Tascosa road. A solitary rider, hunched forward in the saddle on a huge bay.

John Borrasco.

13

Borrasco had outguessed him. He had figured to be at least one day ahead of the
bounty man, but he had been wrong.
Borrasco, in that uncanny mind of his, had
not been taken in by any of the ruses. Ruick
remained in the shadows of the porch, one
thing certain and definite making itself clear
within him. His time in Saddlerock was finished, done with. Despite the facts that
Borrasco would not know for sure he was in
the town and that the natural aversion of
people to bounty hunters might delay his obtaining that information, he would still find
out.

He watched the bounty man ride up to
the Longhorn and swing stiffly from the
saddle. His hunched figure glided across
the porch and disappeared into the inte-
rior. Within minutes he returned, mounted
the bay again and started up the street, toward Ruick, heading apparently for Martin
Gonzales' livery stable.

Ruick drifted deeper into the darkness,
into the narrow passageway between Vaca's
store and its neighbor. Moving quietly as

possible over the accumulation of trash and powder-dry weeds whipped into the corridor by the winds, he finally reached the alley running behind the buildings on the west side of the street. Just as he turned from the passageway, the sound of Borrasco's tired horse was a measured beat a scant dozen yards away. Dan waited until man and beast had passed and then trotted to the back of the hotel. He took the stairs to the second floor two at a time and let himself into the hallway through the narrow door. Moving softly, he eased by Flora's quarters and halted at his own. Ducking inside, he grabbed up his warbag, stowed the few articles he had removed back in it and wheeled about to leave. A second thought passed through him, and, stepping to the bed, he fashioned a figure with the extra blanket and pillow. That completed, he turned again to the doorway.

His fingers froze on the knob. Boot heels were ascending the lobby stair. That would be Borrasco. He waited until he heard a latch click, a door close and a key screech in its lock; he stalled another dragging three minutes for good measure, never for once underestimating the bounty man, and then let himself into the hall. It was dark and silent.

Once outside he descended the stair quickly, swerved off into the shadows and took up a position behind a thin cottonwood on the far side of the yard. From that vantage point he had a clear and commanding view of the hotel's second-floor exit, through which he had just come. If John Borrasco had heard and suspected, he would come through that doorway.

Waiting, Dan Ruick considered his position. Borrasco would do nothing until morning. At that time he would begin his canvass for information. It might take him several hours or it could require only minutes, depending entirely upon where he went first for his answer. That was good; no matter when he got his information, Dan would be gone, riding with Fay Grote and the rest of Dunaway's men somewhere on the Silver Flats — and the bounty man would necessarily have to bide his time until the day was over.

And with a little luck Dan would have found Albert's killer, or at least have uncovered a lead that would permit him to act. He could remain out of Saddlerock until after darkness had fallen and then return, if need be — or he could ride on. All would depend upon what he learned on the Flats tomorrow.

He stirred impatiently. Running from John Borrasco was beginning to be a little tiring. Maybe he should stop, face him, have it out and end it one way or another. And add another killing to his name. He shook his head. Willie Dry, like those before him, had been unavoidable. It was either kill or be killed. With Borrasco it was different. So long as he kept out of the bounty hunter's way, he could sidestep that one. And that he would do — except he was determined to have his one day to find Albert's murderer.

He waited a full five minutes, and, when no one appeared, he retraced his steps along the dark alley to Vaca's store. Moving to the street, he checked it to be certain no one was particularly watching that point and then crossed over to Gonzales' stable.

Locating the roan without disturbing the snoring night hostler, he laid the saddle and bridle on the horse, and, with only a hackamore, led him to the barn at the rear of Dunaway's Lincoln Street house.

Stabling the animal, he momentarily considered the darkened bulk of the building, decided against it and climbed to the loft of the stable. Hollowing out a bed in the sweet-smelling hay, he made himself comfortable and immediately fell asleep.

14

At the first break of daylight Dan awoke. He went down the ladder and entered the hardpack clearing of the yard. Two other men, Crandall and Humboldt, were ahead of him, standing at the bench near the pump, washing the sleep from their eyes with icy water. They watched him curiously but asked no questions, and he volunteered nothing.

Later, at breakfast, he was left strictly to himself, and no mention of the affair with Willie Dry was made, even by Nathan Dunaway, who sat, like a small-time king, at the head of the long, narrow plank table. When the meal — one of steak, potatoes, hot biscuits, coffee in quantity and apparently designed to last a man for a full day — was over, he got to his feet.

"You have the orders," he said in a businesslike tone to Fay Grote. "I want things settled today with both Sharp and McCall. I'll accept no excuses. Understood?"

Grote nodded. He glanced about the table. "All right, hit the saddle!"

They trooped out into the yard to the

133

corral, where their horses were all ready to go. Wordlessly they swung aboard and rode from the house, striking northward.

"Sharp first," Grote announced over his shoulder. "I'll be doin' the talkin'."

Dan trotted the roan in beside the foreman. "When we get close to where my brother was ambushed, say the word. I want a look around."

Grote merely grunted.

They maintained a steady pace across the Silver Flats, following the familiar, well-rutted road that ran along the west border of McCall's land. The morning was crisp and cool, and overhead the sky was an empty, spotless blue arch. It would be a full hour yet before the day's heat began to rise, and the horizon, unobstructed by haze, was a rolling, smooth line in the far distance. Many times Dan had ridden that trail with Albert, the two of them astride the family's old mule, heading for the low, timbered short hills beyond Sharp's Rockingchair spread, where a few deer were to be found and taken to replenish the Ruick larder. It seemed long ago, so many years. But in reality it wasn't far in the past.

They reached the tall twin posts that marked the gate entrance of Sharp's place and turned in. Six riders were coming toward them in the distance, riding a few yards off the road, on their way to begin the day's work. Grote gave his signal, and Dunaway's crew slanted off to intercept them. They came to a halt in a closely spaced line, blocking the Rockingchair riders' way.

Grote said, "End of the line, boys. Sharp's moving off today. You got no job left around here. Just keep on ridin' when you get outside that gate."

Sharp's men stared at Grote's hard-cornered face. One, a youngster with yellowish hair that cropped out beneath his battered Stetson, stiffened.

"The hell you say! Mr. Sharp sure didn't tell us nothin' like that!"

"He don't know it hisself yet," Grote replied with a short laugh. "We're on our way to tell him right now."

"Then I reckon I'll just wait till he says I ain't got a job no more."

"I'm tellin' you now," Grote said in a soft, menacing tone. "You figure to call me a liar?"

The young cowboy started to make an angry protest, but the older man sitting next to him reached out and laid a restraining hand on his arm.

"Forget it, kid. These here fellers are Dunaway's men. I 'spect they know what they're talkin' about."

Grote nodded. "You're smart, old man. Likely you'll live to a real old age. All of you, just keep movin' when you leave here and you won't have no trouble."

"I got me some things back there in the bunk house," another of them began. "I'll just mosey —"

"They won't be worth goin' back for," Grote said coldly.

The cowboy stared at him for a long moment. Finally he shrugged. "No, I reckon not."

Dan pushed the roan forward a few steps, immediately capturing the attention of the Rockingchair crew.

"Name's Ruick. My brother got ambushed out around here yesterday. Any of you got any ideas how it happened?"

He did not actually expect a direct reply; he hoped only for a clue in the reaction the riders might show.

"Didn't even know him, mister," the blond cowboy answered. "Fact is, I didn't know they had been a killin'."

"Yesterday morning," Dan said, and let his glance travel over the others.

Each shook his head. The older man

said, "I knew your brother. More'n that — I knew your folks when you had a place over east of here. But I sure ain't got no idea about who bushwhacked Albert." He swung his eyes to Grote. "All right for us to move on? Sure a far piece to Dalhart."

"Get goin'," Grote said, kneeing his horse up beside Ruick. "And lookin' back won't be healthy."

The Rockingchair crew started forward, circling Grote and his men, and turned into the main road. Once beyond Sharp's gate they put their horses to a gallop, heading for Saddlerock and points further on.

Gordon Sharp was standing on the porch fronting his low, rambling ranch house when they trotted into the yard. He was bareheaded, and the sunlight shone bright silver as it struck his thick thatch of hair. He was coatless, and had evidently got up from his breakfast when he heard their approach. Leaning on his cane, he regarded them with fierce, old eyes.

"What do you want now?" he demanded of Grote.

"You know the answer to that," the foreman drawled. "Dunaway's buyin' this place. We're takin' over this mornin', right now, in fact. Best thing you can do is hitch up that buggy of yours and get to town and sign up with Dunaway."

Sharp bristled. Color mounted in his face, and the corners of his straggling mustache began to twitch. He glanced about the yard, over his shoulder to the bunk house. Inside, where there had been a rattling of pans, there was suddenly silence.

"No use you lookin' for that crew of yours," Grote advised. "They've already took off for somewhere else. Dalhart, I'm thinkin'."

Sharp's defiant face swung back to the riders and settled on Dan.

"Always knew you was no dang good," he exclaimed, venting his rage and frustration on Dan. "This kind of high-bindin' business is right up your alley!"

"Maybe you made friends of the wrong people," Dan said drily.

"I got friends!" Sharp roared, coming off the porch. "Plenty of 'em, and they won't stand for this!"

"Your friends are in the same wagonload of hay as you are," Grote said. "Now, what's it to be? You goin' in and see Dunaway or we just takin' over?"

"Get the hell off my place — that's my answer!" Sharp yelled. "I ain't sellin' to Dunaway or nobody else!"

Grote shrugged his thick shoulders. "All right, boys," he said without looking around. "You heard him. Burn 'er down, the whole kit and kaboodle."

Sharp's face stiffened with alarm. "No — wait — listen to me!"

Dan Ruick's voice was like winter's wind. "I remember another old man, seven years back, praying for somebody to listen to him. You were one of those who wouldn't."

"You just watch," Grote said with a laugh.

Sharp, in a frantic, futile effort, lunged forward and seized the bridle of Grote's horse. The foreman drove spurs into the animal's flanks. It leaped ahead, knocking the old rancher sprawling into the dust. He lay there, motionless, stunned, cloudy eyes not seeing the devastation that was taking shape around him.

Crandall and the others were methodically touching off fires along the buildings, opening gates to release the livestock that were in the corrals and pens. The Chinese cook came running from the back of the main house and took up a position near the corner, where, stoically, he watched Bill Humboldt distribute the contents of a can of coal oil along the porch and then touch a match to it.

Sharp came slowly to a sitting position as the crackle of flames began to grow louder. His eyes once again sought Dan, who, still sitting his roan horse, had taken no hand in the destruction. But there was no acknowledgement of that fact in the rancher's gaze — only hate and accusation.

Ruick favored him with a twisted grin. "Now you know how it feels," he said. "I'm thinking about the time you and some of your crew caught me on your land. Said I was rustling your beef. I wasn't and you knew it, but that didn't keep you from giving me a hiding with a rope. Just so I wouldn't ever be tempted to steal any of your beef, you said. Now — how do you like being pushed around? How do you like being the little man, not strong enough to fight back?"

Sharp's eyes fell, expressing his defeat at last. "Get out of here," he muttered. "Get out of here and leave me be."

Grote leaned forward in the saddle. "Go get in your buggy, old man, and I'll take you in to see Dunaway."

Sharp wagged his head. "Get out of here. I'll go in by myself."

"All right, I'm takin' your word. But if you don't and I have to come lookin' for

140

you again, you'll be mighty sorry you didn't do it!"

Sharp said, "No point in stayin' here."

Grote ducked his head approvingly. "Now you're talkin' sense. And you better figure on the price Dunaway will be payin' to drop a mite. Place with no buildin's on it sure ain't worth much."

Sharp lifted his weary features to the foreman. The entire left side of his face was covered with dust from being knocked to the ground.

"No place is worth much with your kind around," he said.

Grote only grinned. He pulled his horse around and motioned for Crandall and the others to come. Together, as they had ridden in, they started back up the road for the gate. Dan, casting a glance back over his shoulder, felt a twinge of sorrow for old Gordon Sharp and his once fine ranch. It was pretty rough on the rancher, there was no mistaking that. The last glimpse he had of the place was the Chinese cook standing beside Sharp and both watching the leaping flames consume the buildings.

"Now we'll talk to the McCalls," Grote said, as they reached the main road.

15

Nearly an hour later they pulled up in a scatter of low piñon and juniper trees crowning a rise at the lip of an arroyo.

"Here's where your brother got killed," Grote said to Dan Ruick. "We was all just settin' here on this point. Bullet came from somewhere along the wash. Whoever did it, I figure, took out through that thick brush."

Dan surveyed the area with thoughtful eyes. Grote was probably right. A man hiding in the tangle of arroyo growth could easily have fired his fatal bullet and quickly escaped unseen. His eyes caught the bright glitter of brass a few steps to one side. Keeping in the saddle, he moved over, leaned down and picked up half a dozen pistol cartridge casings. Studying them for a moment, he asked, "You say you did or didn't get a shot at the ambusher?"

Grote shook his head. "Couple of us was just doin' a bit of target practicin', that's all. Come on, let's get to the McCall place."

They all rode off the rise and dropped

down to the level run of the prairie. Dan tossed aside the spent cartridges — they were of the common caliber, plentiful over the frontier — and maintained his place in the line. Later he would come back and hunt carefully along the arroyo and see if he couldn't find some item, some clue that would be of help to him. There was very little time left to do anything, he knew. With Borrasco snapping at his heels again, he had to act quickly or give up the idea.

They reached McCall's late in the morning. The rancher and his wife were standing in the yard, eyes on the armada of smoke clouds building in the north and slowly drifting off to the east. The rancher and his wife turned to face Grote and his men, anxiety but no fear on their features.

McCall ducked his head at the dark clouds. "Sharp's?"

Grote nodded. "He sold out. You're next on the list. You plan to be agreeable or do we hand you the same treatment?"

McCall's eyes swung to his wife. She looked very tall and slim in a white housedress. A flowered apron covered the lower half of it, but the upper, fitted closely to her body, revealed her curving youthfulness. Her hair appeared blue-black in the sunlight, and her eyes were almost as dark.

Whatever George McCall had been searching for in his wife's calm features, he apparently found.

He said, "My place isn't for sale. Not under any conditions. I'm asking you to leave now."

Grote lifted his hands and let them fall in a gesture of resignation. "All right. McCall. If that's the way you want it. But you're wastin' your time. Dunaway owns Sharp's, and your water supply comes from there. You don't go along with what he wants, he'll just dam up that creek and leave you high and dry."

"We'll manage. Man can haul his water if need be."

Grote shook his head. "Be quite a chore. And you might have a mite of trouble doin' it." A note of impatience slipped into his tone. "Now, look here, McCall. Don't make this tough on yourself! You got a right nice woman there, and they ain't no sense in makin' it hard for her. Hate to see anything happen to her, too. Use your head!"

McCall took a step forward. "You touch my wife and I'll kill you!" he declared, enraged.

"No call to touch her, once you decide to go along with Dunaway's offer. Up to you."

144

Lilith McCall spoke for the first time. "Just as my husband said, our place is not for sale. All your threats won't make us change our minds."

"You'll be the only ones who ain't sellin' out to Dunaway," Grote pointed out, strangely patient "How long you think you can stand alone?"

"Long as necessary to prove our rights," the rancher replied. "You go back and tell that to Dunaway. Tell him I won't sell and the only way he'll ever get me off this land is to kill me!"

"Well," Grote answered, shrugging, "if that's the way you feel about it, I guess there ain't no other answer."

He shifted slightly in the saddle. Dan saw the bright gleam of sunlight on metal.

"Look out!" he yelled at McCall.

The blast of Grote's pistol shocked the still morning into a crescendo of rolling echoes. Lilith McCall stared at her husband with disbelieving eyes. He stood very stiff and straight, the skin of his face tightening until it seemed stretched over the bones of his face. A frown wrinkled his brow, and then he fell, dead before he struck the ground.

A piercing, far-reaching scream came from Lilith's lips as she dropped to her knees beside him. Her hands went to his face and cupped his cheeks, while small, pleading sounds issued from her throat. She kept murmuring, "No-no-no —" in hopeless denial.

Dan Ruick, no stranger to violence and death in all its shapes and forms, felt sickness sweep over him. What he had witnessed was murder, cold-blooded and simple. Although the rancher had been armed, he had made no visible attempt to reach for his gun. A wave of pity for Lilith McCall moved through him. He swung down from the roan, hearing Grote's raspy voice say:

"You all saw him reach for his iron. And you heard what he said about killin'. Nothin' I could do but defend myself."

Dan met the foreman's insolent gaze. "It was nothing but murder," he said. "Don't try and pull that yarn on me."

He stepped to the fallen rancher's side and dropped beside the quietly sobbing Lilith. He knew McCall was dead, but he verified it nevertheless. He touched her wrist.

"I'll carry him inside for you."

She nodded woodenly, her eyes empty, senses numb. Dan slipped his arms under the body and came to his feet.

"Let him be," Grote ordered sharply. "He asked for it. Let him lay there so's some of the rest will understand we mean business."

"Can't let him lay out here in the yard," Dan answered. "And she can't move him."

"I said let him be!" Grote snarled. "What do I care about him — or her? One thing you'd better get straight, too, lady. We're through foolin' around. Now, I ain't goin' to burn these shacks of yours down like I did Sharp's. I'm givin' you a chance to get your stuff out and leave, but you better be gone by noon tomorrow. You won't get no second chance!"

Dan started for the house. Grote's voice checked him again.

"Put him down, Ruick!"

Dan paused, preparing to place McCall's body back on the ground and face the foreman. There was a definite threat in the man's tone, and Dan was rapidly reaching the point where he would not allow it to go unchallenged.

He heard Beaver Crandall's drawling voice say, "Let him alone, Fay. Woman can't do it alone, and it ain't decent to let him lay out there where she'll have to look at him. I reckon she could use a bit of help from somebody."

There was a long moment and then Grote answered, "All right. Go ahead, Ruick, do your lady friend a turn. But get yourself back to town quick. We got more work to do today."

The tenseness faded from between Dan's shoulder blades and he resumed his slow march toward the house. Lilith followed behind him, neither aiding nor hindering, and he knew she had heard little if anything Grote had said to her. He hooked his toe in the base of the screen door and jerked it open. The house was two rooms, one a kitchen and living room, the other a bedroom. He laid McCall's body on the bed in the latter and stepped back. Lilith sat down in a rocking chair near the head of the bed, and, turning, Dan left the room, leaving her with her grief.

For the past few minutes a strong resentment had begun to build within him. Not because he held any particular grief for George McCall — he had never seen the man before yesterday — nor did he have any sympathies one way or another toward Nathan Danaway's desire to possess all the land. It was simply the way of things, the cold-blooded, merciless way of things — the Dunaways and the Grotes trampling the McCalls underfoot, not hesitating even to take a life in the process.

He heard her crying then, deep wrenching sobs. Shock had finally worn off, realization had clarified her mind and she was letting herself go. Deeply disturbed by the sound, he walked to the tool shed at the far side of the yard. There he got a long-handled spade, and, selecting a shady place on a low knoll just beyond the buildings, he set to digging. He was nearly finished when he became aware of her presence.

She was standing at the edge of her husband's grave, the barrel of a forty-four caliber Henry rifle leveled at his back.

16

Dan continued his work. "I figured you'd want to bury him here, on your own land," he said.

"Get out! Get off this ranch!" she cried in a barely controlled voice. "Get off or I'll shoot!"

Dan turned around slowly. Her face was set, flushed. Grief had puffed her eyes, and the bright sparkle of tears still clung to their edges.

"You'll need some help with him," Dan said gently. "I can help if you like."

"I won't have you around!" she retorted, her voice rising to a shrill pitch. "I won't let you touch him. You're one of them — no better than they are!"

"I don't hold with murder."

"But you were with them."

"For one reason — to find out who killed my brother. No more, no less."

"He was one of them, too!"

"I don't think he knew what they were doing. If you had known Albert, you would realize he couldn't be one of them. I don't think he knew what it was all about."

Dan climbed from the narrow trench and waited beside Lilith McCall. She was trying hard to not break down again and was finding it difficult. He reached forward and took the rifle from her hands.

"No need for this," he said. "I'll go when you want me to, but I would like to help."

She stared at him for a moment and then, wheeling about, walked toward the house. Dan followed. Halfway across the yard he slowed as he saw a rider turn into the gate. It was Gordon Sharp. The old rancher, dusty and soot-marked, was riding bareback and having trouble staying aboard. He pulled to a halt in front of Lilith.

"What's goin' on here?" he demanded.

"George has been shot — killed," she replied in a lifeless voice.

Sharp's eyes blazed. "You!" he yelled, pointing a gnarled finger at Ruick. "You murderin' whelp! I'll see you hung for this!"

"He didn't do it," Lilith explained wearily. "He was with them, but he stayed to help me."

"Didn't see you offerin' any help at my place," Sharp said caustically, sliding off his mount.

Dan shrugged. "Different matter. Maybe

I figured you had no help due you."

"And maybe it was because I wasn't no woman," Sharp added. "Who killed George if you didn't?"

Dan ducked his head towards Lilith. "Mrs. McCall could tell you but I'll spare her the trouble. It was Fay Grote."

"That murderin', sneakin' snake!" Sharp exploded again. "One of these days he's goin' up against the wrong man and get a taste of his own medicine!"

He followed Lilith inside the house. Dan trailed after him, placing the rifle he had taken from Lilith in the corner. She had sat again in the chair at the head of the bed, and was rocking slowly to and fro, making no sound.

"You want me to go ahead with things, Mrs. McCall?" Dan asked. "Or wait?"

"No need to wait," she said lifelessly. "George is gone."

"What about the coroner?"

Sharp broke in. "I'll fix it with Doc Shaughnessy. You go on out in the barn and see if you can nail together a —"

Dan nodded his understanding. In the barn he found the tools and enough lumber to construct a coffin of sorts. When it was ready he carried it back to the house, leaving it outside while he entered.

Sharp glanced inquiringly at him, and he nodded. The old rancher then took Lilith by the shoulders and left, leaving Dan to finish the task.

When he had placed McCall's body inside the crude casket and carried it to the knoll, he waited for Lilith and Sharp. They appeared shortly, and with the rancher aiding him, he lowered the coffin into the grave. Sharp said a few words while Lilith stood by, her hands clasped so tightly the knuckles were white. When that was done, Sharp walked her slowly back to the house while Dan filled in the trench. They were waiting for him when he returned. He was pleased to see she had again got herself under control.

"Thank you," she said as he turned to mount the roan. "It was kind of you to help."

"No thanks necessary," he said. "I'm sorry it had to happen."

"Won't be the last of it," Sharp declared, once more his testy, acid-tongued self. "Dunaway's not going to get away with this!"

Dan ignored him, knowing there was little Sharp or any other of the ranchers could do about the matter. To Lilith he said, "What are your plans, ma'am? You sure can't stay here."

"I can and will," she replied. "This is my home, all I have left now. George died for it — the least I can do is to stay and continue to fight for it."

Dan shook his head. "A fight you can't win. Better you pull out before things get worse. You see how Grote won't stop at anything now."

She leveled her dark eyes at him. "Would you run if it were yours — your only possession?"

Dan Ruick looked away, out across the Silver Flats, now hazy with afternoon heat. "No," he admitted slowly, "I reckon I wouldn't, not if it was me. But that's the difference. I know the Grotes and their kind. I know how to fight them."

"I can fight well as any man, and will," she said coolly. "If they come again, they will learn that. And tell them that when you get back."

Dan threw a glance at Sharp. The old rancher nodded his head. "He's right, Lilith. You can't buck that bunch alone. None of us can. We don't know how to fight them, not the way you have to fight. We need gunslingers like Dunaway hires."

Lilith's eyes settled on Dan. "You aren't

their kind; you said so yourself. Won't you please help us?"

Dan shrugged. "Thanks again, no," he said, thinking of John Borrasco. "I'm not mixing in this any deeper than I already am. Soon as my own job is done, I'll be moving on."

"Ought to know you couldn't expect no help from him!" Sharp said in an edged voice.

"Finding your brother's killer, that what you mean?" she pressed, ignoring the rancher's sarcasm.

"That's it. I thought it might be easier to do working along with the men who were with him when it happened. But I figure now I can do better alone. I'm riding in to collect a little money due my brother's widow and quitting Dunaway."

Gordon Sharp's bushy gray brows came up to a high arch. "Quittin' Nate Dunaway? Boy, you got another guess comin' your way! Nobody quits him, I'm told."

"I will," Dan said quietly, and swung up into the saddle. Removing his hat, he leaned toward Lilith. "I'm sorry for what happened here today. Had I known what he was figuring, I would have tried to stop Fay."

"You did all you could," she said with a

faint smile. "Thank you again, and good-by."

Dan touched the brim of his hat with a forefinger and wheeled from the yard. He hoped she would not persist in her determination to hold the ranch against Dunaway. Grote wouldn't be patient this second time. Perhaps Gordon Sharp would be able to persuade her, but, thinking about it as he jogged along slowly, he knew it was a futile hope. She was the sort who meant what she said. And that was too bad.

But of no real concern to him.

He had his own strong problem, and already he had wasted too much time — something he had very little of. But a man just didn't ride off and leave a woman in the fix Lilith McCall had been forced into, Borrasco or no Borrasco.

He glanced to the sun, estimating the hour. The day was almost gone, but it would still be light long enough for him to look over the spot where Albert had been killed. Perhaps he would turn up something there, something that would give him an idea of whom he was looking for. If not — Well, he would cross that bridge when he got there.

17

Dan rode straight to the knoll where Albert had been slain. He wanted a better look at the ground, to see whether he could find the exact spot where the ambusher had lain. Dismounting, he prowled about in the brush until he found the place where his brother had tumbled from the saddle, brown stains on several rocks furnishing grim evidence. Taking a line from there to the most logical point in the arroyo for a person to hide, he swung back onto the roan and went down into the deep wash.

He missed by only a few feet. Deep in the center of some doveweed and mesquite he found where a rider had halted and waited for some time, judging from the number of hoof prints tamped into the small area. He examined the ground closely, looking for distinguishing marks in the prints or possibly something the killer had dropped. But eventually he gave it up; there was nothing. Afterward he followed the trail left by the murderer, thinking it might lead to some definite place. But that hope faded, too, when the tracks worked up to a rocky shelf and became lost.

Tired and disappointed, he turned the roan toward town as the afternoon shadows began to lengthen. The day was nearly over, and he had learned nothing. But he would not give up, perhaps tomorrow he would uncover something of value, something that would permit him to fulfill the promise he had made to himself to avenge Albert's murder.

But there was John Borrasco to reckon with. Now that the bounty hunter was in Saddlerock, he would be searching for Dan, waiting to shoot him down if need be. Well, he would just have to take his chances on keeping away from Borrasco; he had no choice but to risk it, unless he was willing to abandon the quest for his brother's killer. And that he would not do.

It was full dark when he reached Saddlerock, and there, despite the cover of night, caution laid restraint upon him. He pulled to a halt off the end of Front Street, studying the dusty strip and the few people upon it with infinite care. He did not see John Borrasco's familiar shape among them, yet Dan's inborn caution kept him to the shadows and well off the street while he made his way to Dunaway's place on Lincoln. He felt he would be reasonably safe there. A bounty hunter would make little headway obtaining information from that quarter. He walked the roan into the yard quietly, still alert and trusting nothing to fortune, and tied him to the back side of the corral. The horse was tired and should be fed and watered, he realized, but first he wanted to check in the house and see that all was well.

He crossed the yard, again staying in the darker areas, and entered Dunaway's by a rear door. The cook, in the act of cleaning up his pots and dishes, greeted him dourly.

"Man sets at my table at the right time, else he goes without. You ain't eatin' here tonight."

"My good luck," Ruick said and brushed on by.

He entered the dining room, and was halfway across it when Fay Grote's deep voice in the adjoining parlor checked him.

"Ruick ain't goin' to like it when he hears what Dunaway's pulled. He thought a heap of that brother of his, and Dunaway messin' around with the widow's liable to stir up a real fuss."

"Maybe you ought to tell him you don't like it." Otis Kirby's voice was tinged with sarcasm.

"I done told him," Grote replied.

"Where's he got her and the kid?"

"Upstairs. Says she's thinkin' things over, but I figure he's doin' all the thinkin'."

"He's been doin' a lot of thinkin' about her for quite a spell," Kirby observed with a laugh. "Don't figure he was sorry old Bert got plugged a'tall! Kind of got the husband out of the way so's he'd have a better chance."

Flora and Danny there — in Dunaway's house?

It was unbelievable! They should be miles away by this time. Dan Ruick stood in the center of the room for a long minute, mulling the information through his mind. And then a flood of anger rocked through him as realization came. Flora would not have stayed of her own accord; Dunaway must have forced her in some way. And, putting two and two together, the dislike and fear Flora had expressed for the land buyer and the things Otis Kirby had said, it appeared Dunaway had been trying to have his way with his brother's wife for some time.

That duplicity, the cold-blooded killing of George McCall and his dislike for Nathan Dunaway in general fused suddenly and crystallized in Dan Ruick's mind. He

160

had had all of the man he wanted; he didn't need him or his men to help find Albert's killer; he could do it alone, and he would make that point clear right then. But first, there was the matter of collecting some rightfully due money. That done, he would take Flora and the boy and they would get out of there. It might take a bit of doing, but Dan's temper was at such a peak at that moment that the difficulty of the task did not seem to matter.

He continued on through the dining room then and entered the parlor. Grote, Kirby, Beaver Crandall and Humboldt were at the table, playing cards. The foreman glanced up as he entered.

"You're plenty late," he grunted.

"Been busy," Dan answered briefly. "Where's Dunaway?"

"Why?"

"If I thought it was any of your business, I would tell you," Dan snapped. "Where is he?"

"Now, hold up here —" Grote, angry, started to rise.

Crandall said, "Upstairs. In his office."

Ignoring Grote, Dan pivoted to the stairway. Behind him, Grote's voice continued: "You get finished, come back down here. Got a few things I want to explain to you. Like who's runnin' this outfit."

Dan didn't answer; he continued to ascend the steps. At the top he turned right, down the narrow and dark hallway off which several rooms opened. In one of them were Flora and Danny, he guessed. He reached the end and, halting, knocked.

"Who is it?" Dunaway's muffled voice asked.

"Ruick."

After a moment a key grated in the lock, and the land speculator stepped back to admit him. He had a wide smile on his face, and Ruick had a bad moment during which he wanted to smash his fist into the man's teeth.

"Glad you came up," Dunaway said, closing the door behind him. "Little personal matter I want to discuss with you. Sorry about that deal out at McCall's, but I guess we have to expect such. The boys tell me you stayed to help the widow out. Good idea. Lets them know we're human, just like they are."

He crossed the room and turned up the wick of a large table lamp, bringing more light into the shadowy room. "By the way, there was a man in town today looking for you. Marshal said he was a bounty hunter. Know him?"

Ruick nodded. "I know him." He walked deeper into the well-furnished office. "Dunaway, I'm through," he stated in a rough-edged voice. "I've had all of you and your bunch I want."

"Now — wait a minute!" Dunaway exclaimed, his eyes opening wide in surprise. "What's this all about? That killing at McCall's — that it?"

"I know you've got my brother's widow here. Her and the boy. Dunaway — if you've hurt either one of them, I'll kill you!"

"Hurt them!" Dunaway echoed. "Not for the world, Dan. She's as safe here with the boy as they would be in church. She's a guest, not a prisoner. I simply persuaded her to stay over and think about a little proposition I made to her. I've asked her to be my wife — we would be married after a decent period of mourning, of course. I was hoping I could depend on you to talk to her, help her make up her mind in my favor."

"I know how Flora feels about you," Dan replied. "And I know she wouldn't have anything to do with you under any condition."

Dunaway made a gesture with his hands. "Oh, you know how women are, Dan.

Don't always know their own minds and need a bit of help getting them made up. I'm sure Flora could see the advantages for herself and the boy if she were to become my wife."

"She'll have her advantages, as you call them, and they won't come from you. I heard also you were seeing her when Albert was alive, behind his back. If I thought you had ever laid a hand on her —"

"Never!" Dunaway cried, taking a step away. "It was only as a friend. She will tell you that!"

"I'll ask her," Dan said coolly. "And if her story is different, I'll be back." Raising his gun, Dan retreated to the door and turned the key. "Just so we understand each other," he said, leveling the weapon at Dunaway's belly, "one yell and I'll blow you through that wall. We've got some business to take care of. I'm collecting the money due me."

"Money due you? You only worked a day —"

"I'm not talking about wages. I'm talking about money you owe on the ranch my brother sold you. Or was forced to sell you."

"I paid him the price we agreed on —"

"I didn't agree to it, and, legally, I owned

half of that property. I want five hundred dollars more. Cash. Right now."

"Five hundred dollars! Dunaway echoed. "That place isn't worth it!"

"Maybe it is, maybe it isn't. Beside the point. It's what you're paying me for it. Little like the way you've been doing business, only this time I'm setting the figure and you'll pay it. Now, do you pay up or do we handle this like Grote handled the McCalls?"

"Haven't got five hundred dollars on me," Dunaway began, eying Dan closely.

"That's a lie, and you know it! Come on, dig it up! I haven't got time to stand around and talk."

He took a step closer to Dunaway, who hastily reached inside his coat.

Dan's shotgun adjusted itself. "That better be a wallet you're reaching for," he said coldly.

Dunaway nodded quickly and withdrew a thick leather fold. He extracted several bank notes and laid them on the table. Dan would have preferred payment in gold, but he doubted that Dunaway would have any in the house. At his office on Front Street, probably, but not here.

"Now, I want a receipt showing this was paid to me for that property. Balance due, you can explain it. Then we will both sign. That's just to keep you from saying I held you up and took the money from you."

Dunaway's light-colored eyes flickered. He leaned forward over his desk and, with a pen, scratched out the receipt Dan had demanded on a sheet of white paper. That done, he stepped back. Dan gathered up the bills and paper and stuffed them inside his shirt, never once allowing the shotgun to waver from Dunaway's middle.

"Turn around."

Dunaway wheeled slowly, facing the wall. Dan ripped a strip of rawhide string from the fringe of a table cover and bound the man's hands behind him. Then directing him to lie down on the floor, he tied his feet. While he was preparing a gag to forestall any calls for help, Dunaway managed to ask:

"How far do you think you will get?"

"Far enough," Dan replied, and pulled the cloth tight.

Leaving Dunaway trussed on the floor, he moved to the doorway, opened the panel and looked cautiously into the hall. It was empty. Down below he could hear the muffled run of conversation, the click of chips and an occasional laugh. If they continued to play, all would be well. The next big problem was to locate Flora and the boy and escape from the house before Dunaway managed to give an alarm.

He eased softly into the dark passageway. If one of the men down below decided to turn in, he would mount the stair and they would come face to face. He had to avoid that if at all possible. The slightest suspicious sound could bring the entire crew down on his shoulders.

Moving quietly, he checked the first door on his right. It was unlocked and the room was empty. The next was, too, but the third was locked, the key still in the slot for convenience's sake. Dan turned it carefully, muffling the sound as best he could with his handkerchief. He pushed back the panel and glanced inside.

Flora was sitting on the edge of the bed, the boy sound asleep behind her. Her eyes were wide with fear, but, when she saw it was Dan, her hand flew to her lips and a cry of relief escaped her. Dan motioned for silence and entered hurriedly.

"We've got to get out of here fast," he said, gathering the boy into his arms. "You know anything about this place? It have an upstairs back door?"

Flora said, "I don't know. I've never been here before."

Nothing left but to look. With the boy sleeping soundly against his left shoulder, the shotgun ready in his right hand and Flora at his heels, Dan moved again into the hallway. He stepped quickly to the end of it, a blank wall. There was no door, and the only exit was down the stair past the open archway that looked into the parlor where the crew was playing cards and out the front.

"This may be close," he whispered to Flora, setting the shotgun against the wall. Reaching inside his shirt, he took out the bank notes and gave them to her. "This is the rest of what Dunaway owed you for the ranch."

Flora started to protest, but he silenced her quickly. "Case I get held up here when we start down those stairs, you grab the boy and run. Go to Vaca's store and wait for me. If I don't show by the time the next stage gets in, take it and leave. Tell Vaca I said to help you."

Flora nodded her understanding. Taking up the gun, Dan slipped back to the stairway and started down, slowly, Flora close behind. The sounds lifting from the parlor were louder now, and smoke hung heavily in the foyer where the steps ended. That was a bit of luck he had not counted on; the smoke offered some degree of obscurity.

Halfway down they could see into the room where Grote and the others were playing cards. They were all present, all intent on their game. One more minute was all they needed, Dan realized. If a step didn't squeak, if the boy didn't stir and make some sound, if he or Flora didn't accidently brush against the railing — they would make it. Just one more short minute. A dozen more steps to the front door.

There was a deafening crash in Dunaway's quarters. The man had somehow managed to overturn a chair or some other piece of furniture and thus draw attention. The men at the table came to their feet. End of the line, Dan thought, and whirled to face them.

18

"What the hell?" Fay Grote demanded, coming to his feet. "What's goin' on up —"

"Nobody moves, nobody gets hurt," Dan warned, sweeping the startled men with the muzzle of the shotgun. "All of you — stand easy, just like you are. And keep your hands in sight. We're going out of here."

Grote cursed in a steady, low voice. "I told Dunaway he was a fool to bring that woman and kid here! Told him it'd mean nothin' but trouble."

"Be no trouble if everybody stays put," Dan said softly, coming down the few remaining steps slowly. To Flora he said, "Move ahead of me. Open the door. If there's a key in the lock, put it on the outside."

The girl slipped by him to comply. "No key," she announced, swinging back the heavy panel.

Dan nodded. Keeping the gun leveled at the circle of men, he walked to the door. Flora was ahead of him, outside now on the porch.

"Dunaway's upstairs, tied up," he said to

the men. "Go on up and turn him loose, but the man who tries to follow me through this door gets shot in his belly."

He paused for a moment, eying the men closely, and suddenly stepped outside. Flora yanked the door closed, and they whirled together, off the porch.

"Run for it — for the shadows behind Shaughnessy's office!" Dan said harshly.

They raced across the open ground, the jolting movement awakening the boy. Behind them the door slammed back, and a man — Grote, it sounded like to Dan — shouted something into the night. A gun crashed, but he did not hear the drone of the bullet and from that deduced Grote and the others had not seen which way they had gone. They reached the cover of blackness behind the doctor's place and flattened themselves against the rough boards, both breathing heavily.

"Close," Dan murmured.

Flora made some reply he did not hear. Then she said, "What's next? We can't stay here long. They'll be looking for us."

The gunshot had roused several people along the street. Dan could hear the pounding of boot heels coming from Front Street, heading for Dunaway's house. He was certain that one of them would be John Borrasco.

"We'll wait here a minute. Let these gawkers get by, and then I'll take you to Vaca's. We'll figure from there."

A dozen or so men trotted by, slanting across the vacant lot for the two-storied building that Dunaway occupied. Several were standing before the open doorway, through which lamplight was streaming, and a few others milled about in the yard. Dan waited until nobody else was going by and then started up the passageway between the physician's office and the ladies' millinery shop, heading for Front Street. He came to the end of the corridor and paused.

"Is it safe?" Flora whispered at his elbow.

Dan shook his head. Two men stood in front of the livery stable, one Martin Gonzales, the other John Borrasco. They were engaged in an earnest conversation, which Gonzales punctuated frequently with gestures.

"Dan, is something wrong — something else, I mean?"

"Streets clear," he murmured, "except for a couple of men. One I don't want to meet just yet. We'll wait a bit longer."

172

To reach Vaca's store they would have to cross over and travel almost the full length of town, a comparatively short distance, to be sure, but one they could undoubtedly traverse without being noticed; it was the crossing over that would be dangerous. Yet they could not remain where they were for long. Dunaway's crew would soon be scouring the night for them.

To his relief the bounty man and Gonzales brought their conversation to a conclusion. Both wheeled about and went inside the livery barn. Dan edged a little deeper into the street, watching the building sharply. When he was certain they were somewhere well within the structure, he nodded to Flora, and they walked swiftly to the opposite side. Circling the Longhorn, they continued on down the alley until they had reached the back of Vaca's store. There they halted. Dan located the rear door and knocked, and in a moment the door opened.

"Who is it there?" the old storekeeper asked, peering into the darkness.

"Dan Ruick. And my brother's wife — widow — and boy. I want to talk to you."

Vaca stepped back. "Come in," he said, no particular welcoming note in his tone.

Flora moved by Dan, and they entered

the small, low-ceilinged room. Vaca closed the door and locked it carefully. Dan placed the boy, again awake, on a nearby low couch and turned to the storekeeper.

"I need your help, my friend," he said. "Not for myself, but for Flora and the boy. I've got to get them out of town. Tonight."

Vaca studied the boy thoughtfully. "Why do you not take them if there is such urgency?"

Dan said, "I've got Dunaway's whole bunch on my trail. And another tough customer as well. I try to get them out of here myself, I'll bring Grote and the others down on them, too. You got somebody you can trust? Somebody that will drive them to the next town where they can catch the stage?"

Vaca was staring at Dan. "You do not work for Dunaway?"

"Not as of an hour ago. I quit. What about getting Flora and Danny out of here?"

Vaca nodded. "It can be done. Wait for a moment."

The storekeeper went into an adjoining room. A few moments later the front door closed softly, and shortly after that Vaca reappeared. He nodded to Dan.

"I have sent my cousin for a buggy and

horse. He is one we can trust and will say nothing. He will be here soon."

Dan said, "Thanks, *amigo.* Getting them out of this town will be a load off my back."

"It is nothing. You fight now against Dunaway, do you therefore fight for the ranchers and landowners?"

Dan said, "No, I'm not mixing in that. They're on their own, far as I'm concerned. This was a personal matter I had with Dunaway."

"I see," Vaca said. "But in your disagreement there is help for them nevertheless." He turned then to Flora. "Is there anything you need for your journey, *señora?* For the little one, perhaps? I see you bring nothing."

Flora said, "No, thank you, Mr. Vaca. We didn't have much to start with. We can make out."

"Where will be the best place for her to go where she can catch the stage east?" Dan asked then.

"Eagle Pass," Vaca replied. "My cousin will have them there by daylight."

There was a light tapping at the back door. Vaca moved across the room to a small window and looked out cautiously. "It is my cousin," he said, smiling. "All is ready, *señora*."

He unlocked the door, and Dan picked up the boy to carry him outside. Flora laid her hand upon his arm.

"I wish we could stay, Dan," she said, appeal strong in her voice.

"Not in the cards," he answered kindly. "Just wouldn't work out. Besides, the minute you're in that buggy and out of here, I'll be gone, too, one way or another."

She looked at him sharply. "What do you mean by that?"

He grinned. "Let it pass. Been doing too much thinking lately, I reckon."

He nudged her toward the doorway and outside. She climbed onto the seat of the rig beside Vaca's cousin, whose large teeth gleamed whitely in his dark face. Placing the boy on Flora's lap, he said, "Seems we've said good-by before, but I'll say it again. And good luck."

"Good-by, Dan. Someday ride in to see us."

"Long ride to where you will be."

Vaca was speaking to his cousin, giving instructions in low, rapid Spanish. Dan glanced inquiringly at him.

"All is ready. To Eagle Pass he will take them and no one shall see them leave. He understands."

"Thank him for me," Dan said, "and tell him I'll pay him well. Just get them there in time to catch the stage."

"There will be no pay," Vaca said, stepping back so the buggy could pull out. "A man does favors for his friends. He expects no pay."

The buggy rolled slowly by. Dan caught a last glimpse of Flora's sad, pale face and heard her murmured farewell. He said to Vaca, "Hell, I don't even know your cousin. He ought to let me pay him. That's a long trip."

"Tonight, Dan Ruick, you are my friend. And from this night on. Thus you also are the friend of my cousin — and all those who oppose Nathan Dunaway."

"Like I said, it was a personal matter. And I'll be leaving anyway, soon as I can get to my horse." He said it automatically, quickly, but the words of Higinio Vaca were seeping deep into his consciousness — *friend* — *my friend* — *friend of my cousin.*

"That, as you would say, is not the point," Vaca spoke softly. "It matters only that you no longer are *his* friend. And each one who opposes such evil makes us that much stronger, just as each drop of water fills a bucket to greater depth."

Dan nodded, not sure he understood

and too pressed for time to consider the words. Since the affair at Dunaway's, he no longer had a place of refuge from John Borrasco; in fact, he had acquired new enemies now that he had to avoid. He thought fleetingly of staying with Vaca, of asking the old merchant to hide him out, but he dismissed that idea at once; it would only bring trouble down upon Vaca. And he knew there was no safety for him in Saddlerock; his best bet was the hills.

"I thank you again for your help, my friend," he said to the merchant, extending his hand.

"*Por nada,*" Vaca replied. "There is one thing I must tell you, Dan Ruick. Have care with Martin Gonzales. He has joined with a man who looks for you, a John Borrasco. Even now they search the town."

"*Gracias.*" Ruick repeated his thanks, grinned and wheeled off into the darkness. He had to move, and move fast. Borrasco, Gonzales, Grote and all the others would be combing the town, and he had to make his way through them to reach the roan waiting at Dunaway's place.

He halted suddenly. A bulky figure loomed off to his left. The shotgun came up fast — and then lowered. The sound of a shot was the last thing he wanted at that moment. He waited a long moment, decided the figure had not noticed him and eased off through the shadows toward Barr's building.

"Hold!" the voice of Martin Gonzales was like a trumpet in the still hour before dawn. "Hold or I shoot!"

Dan Ruick ducked low and lunged straight on at the stableman.

19

He was a weaving, dodging shadow hurtling through the blackness of the alley. Gonzales fired, aiming hastily. The bullet went wild, the orange flash of his pistol lighting up the night for a fragment of time. Dan struck him low, driving the point of his shoulder into the man's short ribs. Gonzales gasped with pain and slammed back against the wall of Barr's frame building.

"Borrasco! Over here!"

Dan, jolted back from the impact, caught his balance. Furious at Gonzales, angered at himself, he swung the shotgun like a club. The barrels caught the stable-man alongside the head, and once again he crashed against the saddle shop. But this time he did not remain upright; he sank into a moaning heap. Dan booted the fallen man's gun off into the darkness of the alleyway and whirled about, listening for approaching footsteps. He blamed himself for allowing Gonzales to cry out — he should have expected it and been more careful. The bounty hunter was probably already nearby, and, if he was not, the shot was bound to attract Dunaway's men. He had to get out of there fast.

He took one long step down the alley, figuring to get in behind the Warbonnet and cross the street where he would not be so conspicuous. The roan was tethered at the corral in the rear of Dunaway's place on Lincoln Street, which meant he had to retrace his steps the length of the town and cross over. He halted, sudden revulsion against further flight from Borrasco or Grote or anyone else coming over him.

Running from anything, any man, was not a part of his make-up. Before, keeping out of the bounty hunter's reach had been a sort of game, a match of wits for both of them; now he was tired of it. Why not stand and have it out with Borrasco? Why not settle it once and for all time? The idea appealed to him — and then he remembered Dunaway and Fay Grote, who were also seeking his blood somewhere in the darkness of Saddlerock. That reminded him of his vow to bring his brother's killer to justice before he rode out.

For a brief moment he hung between a desire to fight it out with Borrasco and Dunaway's men and the need to pay up the debt owed Albert and his own conscience; in the end the latter course won out. He could always return and settle with the bounty hunter and any one else who felt he had a call coming.

He started off down the alley, moving at a fast trot but doing so as quietly as possible. One thing was nagging at his mind — why had no one come running up to investigate the shot Gonzales had fired? It wasn't normal. It was almost as though someone had warned others away, making them keep their distance. He reached the back of Fletcher's Bakery and paused there to listen. Saddlerock was strangely silent. He wanted to work his way up the passageway between the bakeshop and the adjoining café and take a look along the street, but he rejected the idea; it would waste too much time — and he could be inviting trouble.

He hurried on, reaching the Warbonnet. He had planned to cross at this point but a new thought occurred to him. He turned instead into the rear entrance of the Longhorn Hotel, proceeded up the hallway and entered the lobby. Nodding to the clerk who glanced up as he walked by the desk, he moved to the window and looked out. Front Street was deserted.

Over his shoulder he asked the clerk, "Where is everybody?"

The man said, "Down by the livery stable. Some sort of ruckus there."

Across the street from the stable, Dan thought, mentally correcting the clerk. Then he strolled to the door and let himself out on the porch. He could see the small knot of men gathered near Vaca's store, and, still moving casually, he sauntered across the street to the corner of the saloon. Pausing for a moment, he forced himself to relax for a moment and then, as though he were a man with nothing but time on his hands, turn slowly about and walk into the shadows lying heavily beside the building.

There his indolence ended.

He immediately broke into a long stride, heading for Dunaway's place. The darkness was cover enough to mask his movements, and he wasted little time keeping to the blacker pools of the night. It was now a matter of getting to the roan and getting out of town; Borrasco and the others would forsake the battered Gonzales and start searching the town, foot by foot, within a few minutes.

Dunaway's house appeared to be deserted, front door still open, lamplight still streaming out onto the gallery. Dan's natural caution again assumed command and laid its restraint upon his haste. He approached the two-storied building in a swinging circle, once again taking refuge in the shadows.

He reached the corner and drifted silently as a summer breeze along the structure's side. At the edge of the yard he stopped, movement near the stable setting little flags of danger to waving within him. But it was only the hostler, the old man Dunaway kept to tend the crew's horses.

Dan avoided him by going completely around the barn and coming in to the corral from the far side. The roan was waiting as he glided though the darkness and yanked the leathers free of the crossbar. He swung to the saddle and doubled back the way he had come. Best to head north, out onto the Silver Flats, and then strike for the Angosturas, he reasoned. John Borrasco was a stranger to the country, and it should not be hard to keep out of his way.

He reined the roan to the left. The big horse obeyed and then suddenly threw up his head, half rearing. Unexpected movement on the right had startled him.

"Ruick!"

Borrasco's raspy summons was like a whiplash streaking out of the blackness.

Dan fired instinctively, quickly. With the crash of the shotgun, the roan plunged off to one side. In that instant the bounty hunter's own weapon bloomed brightly, and Dan felt the warm breath of the bullet against his cheek.

He doubled low over the saddle. Borrasco's thin shape was a wispy, weaving outline in the shadows, only his wide hat appearing solid and of substance. Dan hurriedly swung the shotgun around for a second try. This was the moment, he realized; the time of sparring with the bounty hunter was gone. Borrasco meant to kill him, if necessary, to stop him.

He saw the dark smudge of motion that was Borrasco, bent low, dodging to one side. He fired and, in that identical fraction of a moment, saw the flash of Borrasco's gun again. He felt the solid, searing shock of a bullet, and it nearly wrenched him from the saddle. His hands seemed to go dead and his entire body numb, but somehow he managed to hang on while the roan thundered off into the night.

20

Acting purely from habit, Dan Ruick broke the shotgun, pulled the spent shells and reloaded. His head was clearing with every leap of the roan, and, now that the anesthetic of the bullet's first shock had worn off, he was painfully aware of his wound. His entire left side was warm and sticky, and the arm was numb.

He glanced over his shoulder. In the darkness he could make out no pursuer. But they were there, somewhere. They would be coming. He tried to determine his position, figure out where the fleeing roan, unguided, had carried him. Somewhere north of town, he saw. He was cutting across the Flats in a wide arc. The horse began to blow at that point, and he pulled him down. They reached the edge of a broad arroyo, near the spot where the ambusher's bullet had felled Albert, he noticed. He came to a full stop.

He was lightheaded, and he shook himself impatiently, trying to dislodge the cobwebs seeking to cover his mind. Allowing the roan to rest, he stood upright in the stirrups and searched the rolling land behind him once more. But there still were no signs of followers — but then he suddenly heard the faint drum of running horses. Apparently Grote and the rest of Dunaway's riders were now on his trail, attracted by the shooting. And somewhere near-by would be John Borrasco.

The sound was to the west, and that was encouraging. He sighed wearily. Let them ride on northward; he would wait a few minutes and turn the roan due west, away from the Flats, and hurry to the Angosturas. A man could hide out there indefinitely, if he had a mind to.

He settled back into the saddle, shoulders sloped forward. He was suddenly very tired and the steady, needle-pointed throb in his shoulder was growing into a sullen beat of pain. He kept trying to keep pace with the receding hoofbeats, beyond him now and still going north. But it was a tremendous effort. A couple more minutes and he could safely cross the Flats and reach the safety of the rugged mountains.

He came bolt upright. A new sound had reached him, penetrating his flagging senses. The sharp, metallic click of iron against rock — a horse walking slowly over a graveled surface. It was below him, behind a low rise. At once he knew its meaning, and who it undoubtedly was — John Borrasco. The man was almost inhuman, so uncanny was his knack for guessing exactly what another man would do.

Dan touched the roan with his heels, and the horse started forward, heading down into the soft, sandy floor of the wash. He thanked his good fortune for allowing him to hear that single warning noise that had telegraphed Borrasco's approach. A minute later and the bounty hunter would have topped the knoll and found him, like a sitting duck, out in full view. Now, on the floor of the arroyo, with the soft sand muffling the roan's progress and the clumps of mesquite, buckbrier and doveweed forming a fairly thick screen, his chances for going unseen were good.

He let the roan cover fifty tedious yards and halted. Listening, he heard once again in the distance the sound of Borrasco's cautious approach. It had worked; the bounty man had passed him by, only a few feet away.

He started the roan again, keeping him to a walk. He pointed him down the arroyo, for, trying to reach the hills now with Borrasco somewhere out there on the

Flats, was out of the question. And to the north was Grote and his crew. Safety lay in but one direction — eastward. Clinging to the horn with one hand, clutching the shotgun in the other, he persuaded the tired roan to trot. For him it was pure agony, but the necessity for getting out of the near trap he had been in was all-powerful. He rode steadily on.

His brain began to fog again, and he shook his head continually, trying vainly to clear it. To him, it seemed he was floating along with the roan, slightly above and not actually in the saddle. There was no surrounding world, no hills, no brush, no solid ground — only a void in which he and the roan fled.

Somewhere in the unfathomable blackness a yellow spot appeared. It drew nearer and grew steadily larger until, at last, it was large as a man, as tall, twice as broad. Savagely he shook his head, struggling to comprehend. He was still on the roan. They had come to a stop before a place that was vaguely familiar. He stared at the rectangle of light, at the indefinite figure in its center; fear brought the wavering shotgun up to an unsteady level.

"Who is it? What do you want?"

A woman's voice. He tried to form a

reply but no sound would issue from his stiff lips. He tore his cramped, clutching hand from the saddle horn, possessed by some vague notion to remove his hat. The next instant he was falling.

21

Dan came awake with a start. His sudden movements sent a stream of pain coursing down his left arm and side; he forgot his desire to sit up and settled back down. He was in a room, the one into which he had, the previous day, carried the lifeless body of George McCall. He was lying on the same bed on which he had put the rancher. His arm was bandaged and smelled strongly of some sort of medicine.

From the doorway leading into the adjoining room Lilith McCall said, "You've had a long sleep."

Dan considered her words. "How long?"

"Since last night. And it's afternoon now."

Denying the pain, he drew himself up to a sitting position. "Can't stay here," he muttered. "Mean only a lot of trouble for you."

"Maybe. But you're in no condition to travel. You lost a lot of blood, but the wound wasn't too bad. The bullet went through without hitting bone. Last night, when you fell from your horse, I thought you were dead."

Dan lowered himself to the pillow again, slowly and gently. Quick movements made him dizzy, and he hadn't realized how weak he was. Must have really lost a lot of blood, as Lilith McCall had said.

"Anybody stop here looking for me?"

"A man. Thin and sharp-faced. Rode into the yard early this morning and looked around for a spell. Didn't ask any questions, though. Just turned around and left."

That would be John Borrasco. "He see my horse?"

Lilith shook her head. "I put him in the cowshed last night. Didn't think anybody looking for a horse would bother to look there."

Smart girl, Dan thought. And a pretty one, despite the lines and traces of sorrow still clinging to her features. He couldn't involve her in any more trouble. "Come dark, I'll saddle up and get out of here," he said.

Lilith moved into the room and stopped at the bedside. She examined the bandage on his arm, felt his forehead and stepped back. "Maybe tomorrow, but not tonight. You've got to have more rest and some good food. I managed to make you eat some hot broth early this morning, just so you could keep up your strength. There's more ready now, and tonight you will have steak and potatoes. Think you can handle the broth if I bring it?"

Dan nodded. "And a cup of black coffee." He wasn't really hungry but knew he needed the food if he were to get back on his feet quickly. And the coffee — most of all he needed a few swallows of strong, black coffee.

She brought it in at once, a thick mug, steaming hot. He took a deep swallow, winced at the scalding temperature and grinned at her. She said nothing, her face serious, and turned once again to the next room. When she reappeared she was carrying a bowl of the broth.

She waited until he drained the cup, took it from him and, after putting it aside, began to spoon the broth into his mouth.

"Figure I can feed myself," he said, half in protest.

She paid no attention to him but continued to ladle out the broth, which, with the strong coffee, began to have its effect.

"Little hard for me to figure," he said when the bowl was empty, voicing a thought that had come into his mind, "your taking all this trouble for me, I mean."

She met his gaze squarely, her own eyes dark and cool. "I pay my debts. You were kind, and did me a favor yesterday when my husband — was killed. I am repaying that favor. Anyway," she added, "you must not be one of Dunaway's men after all. Else why are they hunting you? Why did you get shot?"

"It wasn't —" Dan began, and then fell silent, a strange reluctance to tell this calm, dark-eyed girl about the shadows in his past coming over him.

She watched him closely for a long moment, waiting for him to finish, and when he did not she murmured, "I see," and left the room.

He fell asleep almost immediately after that, and when he once more opened his eyes it was fully dark. He sat up, feeling much stronger. The room was in deep shadow, the only light coming in from the adjoining one, where he could hear Lilith McCall going about her work at the cookstove. Smells of frying meat and potatoes, boiling coffee and biscuits filled the small house, and he discovered he was hungry, ravenously so. He moved to the edge of the bed, noting for the first time that he had been disrobed, and pulled on his clothing, which had been hung over the back of a rocking chair.

The effort made him somewhat giddy, but he brushed the feeling aside and got to his feet. It took a moment to straighten matters out in his mind, but he finally got his bearings and walked in to where Lilith was finishing up the chore of preparing the meal. She did not hear him approach, and for a minute he stood there, regarding her slender, capable figure. Having a man's full appreciation for such, he felt it would be a fine life for a man, having a woman like Lilith for a wife, having a spread like the C-Bar-C. A man wouldn't need much more with such possessions, he thought. His life would be nearly complete.

Only a man had to fight and fight hard for such good things. They never came easily — *no hay ataco, sin trabajo* — he remembered an old proverb Higinio Vaca liked to quote. It meant, "nothing good comes without hard work." It was true in all things, he realized. If a man wanted something like Lilith and his own piece of land, he had to fight for them. And, if he desired them enough, he would. George McCall had tried, but he wasn't one of the strong ones; now he was dead. Would he, given the same opportunity and being caught up in the same situation, be able to hold his own? Perhaps he would and possibly he might not; one thing was certain — he would fight until he, too, were dead if ever he had the opportunity and the stakes were Lilith and a fine little place like the C-Bar-C — and peace.

She half turned and caught sight of him at that moment. Her face was flushed from the stove's heat, and her blue eyes were very dark in the lamplight's glow. A wisp of hair had come loose and was tumbling down over her forehead, giving her a very youthful appearance. She gave him a direct glance and brushed her hair back with an impatient sweep of her hand.

"Afraid I'm causing you a lot of trouble," he said apologetically. It didn't seem right to be imposing on Lilith when she probably preferred to be alone with her grief.

"No trouble," she said. "I like to cook — and it keeps me from thinking. Sit down and I'll get you some coffee. Feel better?"

"Good enough to fork a bronc," he answered, and sat down at the oilcloth-covered table. "Shoulder is a little stiff. Outside that I'm all right."

"After we eat I'll massage it and treat it with hot cloths. The bullet went through the fleshy part of your arm. Not much damage."

"Always was a lucky cuss," Dan said.

She placed the cup of steaming black liquid before him. He drank it down gratefully, feeling better by the moment.

"You made any plans about leaving here?" he asked then.

"No," she replied. "And I won't. My place is here, and here I will stay."

"Be hard to do. Dunaway won't quit until he's got all the Silver Flats country. Why, I don't know for sure. But he's determined to own it."

Lilith turned to him, surprise in her eyes. "You really don't know?"

Dan shook his head. "Oh, I know he's got a customer for it. What I don't get is why this customer is so set on having the whole country. There's plenty land other places."

The meal was ready, and, after placing a heaping platter of food in the center of the table, she sat down opposite Dan.

"There's a foreign syndicate — Scotland, I think — that plans on coming here next year. Their representative has chosen the Silver Flat country as the place they want to set up cattle-raising on a big scale. Dunaway found out about it. He has a friend somewhere in the East who tipped him off."

"And his idea is to move in ahead of them, get hold of the land any way possible and end up in a position to deal with them on his own terms."

Lilith nodded. "At the price he has been forcing the ranchers to sell to him for, he stands to make a huge fortune."

It all fitted into place in Dan Ruick's mind now — the reasons for Dunaway's ruthless methods, the reason he went to the trouble to own the law in the Silver Flats country. To accomplish his purpose and ambition, he had to be the most powerful man in the entire area. Thus, those who opposed him were utterly helpless to fight; with the law on his side and men like Grote to carry out his orders, ordinary people did not have a chance. He understood other things, too — the way Higinio Vaca and Lockhausen and some of the others felt about him. He was a man who could have helped, who understood how to fight the Grotes of this world — but instead he had lined up with Nathan Dunaway and his gunslingers.

He stared thoughtfully at his plate. "Will the ranchers around here stay and fight?"

Lilith moved her shoulders slightly. "Hard to say. They aren't the shooting kind, and they all have families. Maybe, if they had a little backing up, they might."

Dan poured himself a third cup of coffee from the enamel pot. He was beginning to feel like his old self again. Except for a sharp twinge in his arm when he moved it too quickly, the effects of Borrasco's bullet were negligible. Dan's immense vitality, born of living roughly in the outdoors, day and night, was a wellspring pumping a never-ending vigor into his body. He rolled himself a cigarette and watched Lilith begin to clear the table preparatory to washing the dishes.

This was not his fight, a voice seemed to tell him, and long, bitter experience had taught Dan Ruick it was never wise to take a hand in another man's trouble. But, somehow, it touched him, and he could not shake the feeling that it was his fight, too, that he could not allow Nathan Dunaway to get away with selling out the Silver Flats to a syndicate or any other combine who might come in and take over the area. Perhaps it was because it once had been his home, the only one he had ever known, or possibly it was that inner instinct that lies within every man to take the part of the weak against the bullying strong. Or it may have been Lilith McCall. He knew he had no right to think of her —

it wasn't even decent — and he justified it in his outraged conscience by telling himself he could not stand by and see a lone, helpless woman, courageous and determined though she was, manhandled and overrun by Grote and Dunaway.

And, of course, there still was the matter of Albert's killer, which had somehow slipped back into the further corners of his mind. That was his real reason for being here, and forget it he would not. But it all tied up into a single package; accomplishing one would undoubtedly bring about the completion of the other.

"Take off your shirt," he heard Lilith say. She placed a pan of boiling water on the table and dropped several folds of cloth into the bubbling liquid. "I'll try and loosen up those muscles."

Dan removed the garment, washed and mended by Lilith while he slept. She fished out one of the pads, allowed it to cool for a moment and then placed it on the back of his shoulder. The heat was strong, and he winced, grinning a little at her.

"The hotter it is, the better for you," she said firmly.

He settled back, feeling the heat drill into his body, loosening the muscles, warming the bones, filling him with a relaxed, eased comfort. Later, when she was done with the steamy applications, she began to massage the area, gently at first and then with strong, sure hands that set his skin to tingling sharply.

"You should have been a doctor," he said when she at last handed him his shirt.

"I was a nurse, once," she answered. "A long time ago, before I met George Mc-Call."

Dan moved his arm about, exercising it experimentally. "Feels almost like I'd never been shot. I'll get off your hands now."

Lilith shook her head. "No need to leave now — it's late. Tomorrow morning will be soon enough, and you should have one more night of rest and sleep."

He considered that for a moment. It made sense. "It's a deal, but I won't take your bed again. You need rest, too, and I can make out in the barn."

"There's no need —" she began, but he cut off her protest.

"Been thinking about this Dunaway mess. I've got no call to stand by him. I'm around here for one reason — to find out who killed my brother. I can do that from either side of the fence."

Lilith glanced at him, a frown pulling down her full, dark brows. "So?"

"I'll make a deal with you and the other ranchers. I'll help you stop Dunaway — and for that you turn over the man who murdered my brother. I know the ranchers, and probably even you, know who it is. I'll agree to not settle things my own way — I'll just turn him over to a U.S. marshal to see he gets a fair trial. Main thing, I want to see whoever it was brought to account for what he has done."

Lilith did not reply at once. She studied his square-cut features for several moments, and then her glance shifted to his bandaged arm. "What about that — the man who did it, I mean?"

He had not fooled her at all, he realized. "A little personal matter I can take care of," he said with a shrug. "Means keeping out of sight until we could have a showdown with Dunaway and his crowd. No need for you to worry about it. Now, can you get word to the other ranchers to come here for a meeting? I want all of them to give me their word on my offer."

"I can ride to Brunk's. He can spread the call from there."

Dan shook his head. "Don't like the idea of your riding across the flats at night. No hired help left you can send?"

"All gone," Lilith said with a short

laugh. "Grote and his crew saw to that. But don't worry. I can take the back trail, across my own property. No one will see me — or bother me."

"Could go myself," Dan said then. "Fact is, the ride would do me some good."

"It would also get you shot," Lilith said, turning to take her jacket and scarf off a hook. "Far as Brunk and the other ranchers are concerned, you work for Dunaway. None of them would let you get within fifty yards of their places."

That was a fact, Dan had to admit. But he still didn't like the thought of Lilith going off alone. "Why don't I ride with you, sort of stay behind —"

Lilith gave him a brief smile. "Stop worrying about me! I'm a big girl, even a married one. Or was. You stay here and get your rest — you'll need it if the ranchers take you up on your offer. When do you want to hold this meeting?"

"First thing in the morning. Tell them to bring their hired hands along, and be wearing their guns."

She nodded and turned to the door. Reaching it, she hesitated. "Suppose Grote comes here tonight. What will you do?"

"He won't find me, unless he looks in the barn loft."

She started to protest, saying he needed more rest in a comfortable bed, that he was not fully recovered. But he brushed her protests aside.

"Just think what your rancher friends would say, and think, when they come riding in here tomorrow morning and find we'd both been sleeping in the same house!"

Lilith blushed and whirled away. Pulling two blankets from a corner shelf, she handed them to him and again moved to the doorway. "Good night," she said.

Dan took up his shotgun and the two blankets and followed her out into the star-filled, warm evening.

" 'Night," he said. "You're not back here in two hours, I'm saddling up and coming to find you."

"I'll be back," she said, and headed for the stable.

And she was. Dan remained awake until he heard her ride into the yard, put up her pony and enter the main house. Only then did he stretch out on the crisp, fragrant hay, with the blankets around him, and fall asleep.

22

There were five men in the group that morning. They stood in Lilith McCall's small kitchen, sipping black coffee, faces solemn, plainly ill at ease and troubled. Three of them Dan knew — Gordon Sharp; Leo Brunk, who had grown much heavier with the years; clean-shaven, wiry John Heggem. The other two, introduced as Buster Clagg and Joe Harley, were newcomers of only five years' duration on the Silver Flats.

Four other ranchers were invited, but, when eight o'clock came and they had not put in an appearance, Ruick decided to wait no longer. He placed his empty cup on the table and faced the men, who had gathered in a small, tight group on the opposite side of the room and were talking among themselves.

"Mrs. McCall has told you my proposition, I take it," he said. "You being here, I assume you are for it."

Gordon Sharp stepped forward. "Not so's you'd notice it," he said, raising his hand. "We just come along to find out what this is all about. Tell you the truth, Ruick, it don't make much sense, your offerin' to fight for us."

"What made you change your mind?" Heggem asked. "Yesterday you were working for Dunaway. Today you're willing to go against him. Don't make sense."

"Sounds like some kind of a trick to me," Buster Clagg muttered doubtfully.

"No trick to it," Dan replied. "When I blew into town Dunaway offered me a job. Under the circumstances, and at the time, it looked like a good thing to take it. Since then I've learned a few things and I quit. It's that simple."

"You mean you didn't know who Dunaway was and what he was up to?" Sharp demanded.

"Didn't know and didn't particularly care," Dan answered. "Any of you had taken the trouble to tell me instead of just jumping to conclusions, I might have done different. But you are all just like you were ten or fifteen years ago — bull headed and proud and too all-fired good to talk to a man. Anyway, that doesn't mean a thing now. You all know the main reason I hired out to him was so I could find out who shot my brother."

"Ah, yes, your brother Albert," John

Heggem said in a thoughtful way. "I recall, Dunaway didn't have much trouble buying him out. No trouble at all."

Anger rose swiftly in Dan. He threw a quick, hard glance at the rancher, and hot words rushed to his lips. Lilith McCall's calm voice cut them off.

"That hardly seems to me to be the subject here," she said. "Mr. Ruick has offered to help in our fight against Nathan Dunaway. His price is that we turn over to him the name of the person who killed his brother. All we have to do is decide if we will take his offer."

"Got a hunch we'd be making a big mistake," Leo Brunk said. "Sort of wonder if, well, if we can trust —"

Again anger surged through Dan. Lilith caught his eye and frowned slightly, shaking her head. Old ideas, old impressions die hard; they were giving him credit for nothing, only remembering the way of things long past.

"You say you'd help fight Dunaway — lead the fight, I think it was. Right down to the finish," said Clagg. "And for that you'd want us to tell you who shot Albert?"

Dan said, "That's it. All I want out of it."

"Purty high price," Gordon Sharp observed. "You wantin' us to turn over one of our own people to you so's you could gun him down. I say no to that right now. I'll go along with payin' a cash price, a bounty fee, but I won't agree to that other."

"Then we've got no deal," Dan said impatiently. "My gun is not for hire. Never has been. Maybe you've had that idea, along with a lot of others, about me and the rest of my family, but that one's wrong."

Sharp grunted. "Why should we tell you who ambushed Albert, anyway? One of Dunaway's bunch shot George McCall. Right down in cold blood. How about you turnin' that man over to us?"

"You know who it was," Dan said evenly. "And in this country a man kills his own snakes. You want to square matters with Grote, go after him same as I'm going after the man who murdered my brother."

"You figure we got a chance against Dunaway's bunch?" asked John Heggem.

"Depends on how bad you want to keep your land. If you want it bad enough to fight when the showdown comes, I figure we've got better than an even chance."

"Don't know about that," Sharp, ever contrary, said. "Grote and his bunch are all gunfighters. None of us here done much shootin' in the last few years. And the hired hands all backed out, to the last man. You'd about be standin' all by yourself against them."

"We'd do all right," Dan assured them, "long as you will take a gun and fight. Main thing is we've got to buck Dunaway, show him you are all ready to fight for your places. That will give him a little different idea about things."

Sharp wagged his head. "Don't know about that. He won't give in easy. And there's always Fay Grote to reckon with. He'd as soon shoot a man down as bat an eye. Oh," he added, throwing a hasty glance at Lilith, "I'm sorry to be mentionin' that."

The girl said nothing. Dan looked through the window, at the steadily approaching day.

"Getting late. Lets get this thing settled."

"One thing I'd like to know," the small man named Joe Harley said, "is just how you planning to go about this? You figure to plain up and pick a fight with Dunaway and Grote and shoot it out? That it?"

"Be the best way to handle Dunaway," Dan said. "He'd understand that, and so would Fay Grote. But we'd be no match for them in a showdown like that."

"Then how you goin' —" Sharp demanded, and halted as Ruick silenced him with a wave of his hand.

"Get word to Dunaway you'd like to talk things over with him. Set a place, say, Heggem's. He'll figure you're all ready to sell out. All of you be there, and have a lawyer along, one you can trust. Then leave the rest to me."

"What makes you think Dunaway will take the bait?" Sharp asked doubtfully.

"He wants to wind up this business fast. Heard him say so. I figure he'll jump at the chance to get you all together and close the deals."

"And you'll be there?" Heggem asked.

"I'll be there."

Brunk shook his head. "I don't know. Dang it, it could be a trick of some kind. Get us all together and —"

Surprisingly enough, it was Gordon Sharp who broke in with, "No, no, it ain't no trick. I think Ruick's got somethin' here. Only thing I don't like about it is his price." He lifted his eyes to Dan. "Just what'd you have in mind to do with him, once we turned him over to you?"

Dan shrugged. "First I thought I'd give him a chance to shoot at a Ruick who could shoot back. Guess now I've cooled off enough to do it right — turn him over to the law for a trial."

"To Harvey Wilde, that the law you mean?"

"No, a U.S. marshal."

For the first time in several minutes Lilith spoke up. "I think we've all decided Dan's — Mr. Ruick's idea is the answer to the problem. I say we agree to his terms."

"But I don't see how we can —" John Heggem began, and stopped.

There was a drum of hoofs outside, a rush of horses into the yard. Sharp hobbled to the door and peered out. He turned back, his face draining of color.

"Reckon we ain't got time to decide on anything. Here's Dunaway, Grote and the whole bunch!"

23

There was dead silence in the small room. Brunk swung his glittering, angry eyes at Dan. "This some of your doing? You have this set up with Dunaway?"

Dan withered the rancher with scorn. "Don't be a fool," he snapped.

"Hello!" Nathan Dunaway's voice came in to them. "Hello inside that house!"

Dan glanced to Lilith. "Stay in here," he said. "Get down on the floor if any shooting starts." To the ranchers he added, "Stay put, unless I call you."

"Dan!" Lilith cried as he started for the door. "You can't go out there alone!"

He had to, and he knew it. It suddenly was necessary for him to prove to Sharp and Brunk and all the others that they were wrong about the Ruicks — about himself. He gave Lilith a bitter, tight smile and stepped out into the yard.

They were drawn up in a line, facing him — Dunaway, Fay Grote, Humboldt, Beaver Crandall and Otis Kirby, and two more who were strangers to him. Dunaway's eyes showed surprise when he saw Dan.

"Well, now," he exclaimed, "look who we got here, boys! I figured you were a long ways from here, Dan."

"Told you he didn't hole up in the hills," Fay Grote said. The fingers of his right hand, resting on his thigh, began to spread slowly.

"Don't do it, Fay," Dan said with a sardonic grin. "It'll be a good way to get blasted out of the saddle!"

Grote's fingers immediately stopped moving.

"And what do you figure the rest of us will be doing all that time?" Dunaway said, pressing the point. "Just sitting here watching?"

"One good thing about a scattergun," Dan replied easily, "is that buckshot pellets sure splat out. At this range I figure I could put lead in all of you, using both barrels. Now, what do you want around here?"

"Got some papers for the widow to sign. And got her money right here, too."

"She says she won't sell out. Same as the others. Guess that's the answer to that."

Dunaway studied Dan for a long minute. Then, "Well, Fay, looks like we've got some more work to do."

The big man grunted. "Reckon it might

as well start now," he said, and came up with his pistol.

The blast of Dan's shotgun ripped across the morning quiet. Dan fired as he lunged to one side, and his shot went wild even as did Fay Grote's. Someone yelled, the rider to the left of Grote, as the buckshot plowed into his body. Dan fired the second barrel, as the horsemen scattered like chickens under a plunging hawk, and raced for the stable. He needed the protection of the structure's walls, if he was to face them all. And he wanted to draw them away from the main house — away from Lilith.

Inside the small house, Lilith McCall had watched Dan move out into the yard and take up a stand facing Dunaway and the others, one lone figure against half a dozen or more hardened gunmen. She listened while he talked, while he threw down his challenge — for her sake, she realized — and suddenly the hopelessness of his position against such odds struck her.

"We've got to help him!" she cried, facing the ranchers. "We can't let him stand out there alone — and fight them for us. He hasn't got a chance! He's doing it for you — for each of you, can't you understand that? You going to let him fight your fight alone?"

"By God, no!" Gordon Sharp exploded. "This place got a back door?"

She said, "No, but there's a window." She wheeled and led them into the other room. Brushing aside the curtains, she lifted the sash. "You can get out this way."

"Maybe I can," Sharp muttered, "if this dang leg of mine will behave. Ain't goin' to be big enough for Brunk, though. That mean's he's elected to stay in here and watch out for you."

The older rancher clawed himself through the small opening Heggem was close behind him, and then the new man, Joe Harley.

"We'll stand by the door," Brunk said.

Then they heard the thunder of Ruick's shotgun, followed almost in the same instant by a pistol shot. And then the second barrel of the shotgun.

"Scatter!" Sharp commanded, taking charge. "We get them centered here in the yard we got 'em! Everybody pick out somethin' to hide behind!"

Dan raced across the open ground lying between the main house and the barn, reloading as he ran. His arm was giving him some trouble, throbbing a little from the action near the house and now from the jolting of his running. Bullets began to whine past him, to dig into the hard-packed ground, shooting up little spurts of dust where they hit. He started to change course, to dodge and provide as difficult a target as possible. Voices were filling the air, the strident, commanding shouts of Nathan Dunaway, the hoarse replies of Fay Grote. From the corner of his eye he caught motion off to his left. Alarm sped through him. They had encircled him, were cutting him off before he could reach the stable.

And then he saw it was Gordon Sharp, loping painfully on his bad leg for a tool shed standing about halfway between barn and house. The old man had his pistol out. His face was set, and his jaw jutted forward in a determined manner. Looking further, he saw Heggem and Joe Harley, each hurrying to a place of vantage. He swore softly under his breath. They should have stayed inside with Lilith; he had meant for them to protect her.

Riderless horses were trotting off toward the pole corral on the east side of the house. Dunaway and his men had quit the saddle. They would be fighting on foot now, which would be to their advantage and create new problems for Dan. A gun opened up from the doorway of the main house, and this worried him afresh. Whoever the fool was — didn't he realize he would draw fire to himself, and consequently to Lilith?

He threw a hasty glance over his shoulder. Dunaway and Beaver Crandall were standing tight against the wall of the house, eyes on the doorway. Two men were running across the yard, shooting as they came. Half turning, Dan fired his right-hand barrel at the nearest. The man yelled and went down in a heap, clutching at his leg. The other veered sharply. There were only four of Dunaway's crew in sight — where were the others?

Sharp started to fire at that moment, giving Dan a moment of respite from the bullets dogging his tracks. He was only a dozen strides from the stable now, and he wasted no time in dodging. He drove on in a straight, fast line. Once inside he could look out upon the yard; he could climb to the loft, if he so desired, and command the entire area from above.

He reached the partly open door and ducked inside just as Dunaway's men began once more to bear down on him. With bullets thudding into the thick walls, he yanked the door closed and dropped the bar into place. He decided the place where he could be the most effective was upstairs. It would be much easier to see what Dunaway would try to do and also allow him to provide better protection for Sharp and the others. He wheeled to mount the ladder nailed tight against an inner wall.

" 'Mornin', Ruick," John Borrasco's cold voice said from the shadows. "Figured you'd be comin' in here."

24

Dan wheeled at the sound, his gun coming up fast.

"Don't try it!" the bounty hunter warned softly from the depths of the stable. "You're a mighty easy target where you're standin'. Just lean that scattergun against the stall there."

A gusty sigh passed Dan's lips. Another thirty minutes was all he had needed — so close, yet so far. He placed the shotgun, as he had been ordered, against a nearby wall and waited out the moments. After a while Borrasco's thin figure disengaged itself from the shadows and moved out into the open. He halted several feet away, taking no chances. A half smile crooked his lips.

"Still carry that forty-one tucked inside your shirt? Fooled me with that one time, I recollect. Now, just take it out, easy-like and drop it on the floor."

Dan reached slowly for the weapon and dropped it to the litter on the stable floor. He faced Borrasco.

"Was hoping I could stay clear of you for one more day," he stated. "What's next?

Dunaway's not caring much who he shoots. We step out that door, we're both dead."

Borrasco cocked his head, listening to the sporadic firing, the occasional thunk of bullets into the barn's walls.

"We'll wait," he said finally. "They'll come lookin' to see what's happened to you. Then I'll say my piece. You sure got yourself a real ruckus goin'! What's it all about?"

Dan explained, faint hope coming alive within him. If he could persuade the bounty man to hold off, to wait until things could be settled with Dunaway, he wouldn't mind going back with him so much. When he finished Borrasco shrugged.

"Country's plumb full of polecats like this here Dunaway. Somebody ought to declare bounty on them. Probably do a heap of good. Say," he added suddenly, "obliged for your lookin' after Jake back there in Tascosa. He was some tired. Fretted me no end, layin' there in that bed, thinkin' about him out there in the sun."

Dan nodded. "Glad to. Borrasco, I'll make you a deal. Let me wind up this business with Nathan Dunaway and his bunch out there — then I'll ride back with you.

220

Give you my word I'll cause no trouble. Lot of people around here that's going to get hurt if somebody don't stop him."

"Includin' a fine-looking little woman that's now a widow, I take it. That Dunaway do in her husband?"

"One of his men, name of Grote. Never gave him a chance. You could lend these people a hand if you were thinking right. It's me alone against Dunaway's gun-slingers, more or less. These ranchers are all old and not much good with guns."

Borrasco said, "No call for me to stick my hand in a scrap like this. And I can't figure what's got you so all-fired riled up about it. This thing happens every day."

"I grew up around here. Sort of my country. Never thought much about it until I came back by and found my brother had been bushwacked and this Dunaway trying to move in on his own terms."

"One of Dunaway's bunch kill your brother?"

Dan shook his head. Outside the shooting had lulled considerably. Someone was shouting, unintelligible words that could not be understood. "One of the ranchers did it."

Borrasco gave him an odd look. "So you're fightin' for them? Don't make sense."

"My deal was I would fight Dunaway for them if they would turn the man who killed my brother over to me when it was done with."

The bounty hunter said nothing. He was studying Dan's face in the gloom of the barn, turning some problem of his own over in his mind.

"I follow a man clear across the country," he said finally, "then, when I catch up, I turn him loose to take a hand in a land war. That don't make sense either."

"You get your bounty money whether I'm dead or alive. What difference does it make to you? You win either way."

"Been some changes since you last heard," Borrasco said. "That gambler friend of yours added five hundred dollars to the reward money for you alive. Was a thousand either way. Now, to collect me fifteen hundred, I got to get you back alive."

Ruick stared at him. "Tilton did that? Why?"

"Reckon he's a pretty good friend of yours. Seems they's some new evidence he dug up that's in your favor. You do him a good turn some time or other?"

"Once," Dan said. "You telling me the truth?"

Borrasco shrugged. "I'm going to get you back there for that trial alive, ain't that proof enough?" He halted, listening. "Sure got quiet out there."

The bounty man moved by Dan, keeping well out of reach. He stopped at the door, pushed it open a crack and looked out.

"Well, your little widow ain't got no house left. They're burnin' it down. And they're startin' to drag up some brush to stack against this here barn."

"Is —" Ruick began anxiously.

"Is the little widow all right? That what's botherin' you? Reckon she is. She was standin' out there in the yard. Couple of men on the ground that looked like they was done for. A big man, fat. And a towheaded cowboy."

Leo Brunk. And the towhead would be Otis Kirby. It had not been Kirby he had shot while crossing the yard. One of the ranchers must have accounted for him. That cut down the odds a bit. The thought of Lilith standing out there alone, watching the destruction of her home, of death in its most brutal aspect, filled him with a new, burning anger.

He swung on Borrasco. "What about it? You got my word I'll turn myself over to you when this is done with. Do I get to help these people or don't I?"

The bounty hunter hesitated for only a moment. "This is a damn fool stunt on my part, but I reckon it's important to you. Pick up that scattergun and let's get started. I'm going along just in case. Didn't trail you clear across the county just to let some two-bit saddle warmer put a slug in your brisket!"

Dan gave him a brief, appreciative grin. He snatched up the shotgun, reloaded it and gathered a handful of spare shells.

"How we doin' this?" Borrasco asked, checking his pistol.

"Only way we can. Go out that door shooting. Only don't hit the wrong people."

"Could get up in the loft and do a little sharpshootin'," Borrasco suggested.

"Too late for that now," Dan answered. "I smell smoke. They've got this barn set afire."

The bounty hunter sniffed. "Reckon you're right. Come on, let's go," he added, and, stepping to the door, kicked it wide.

The first man Dan Ruick saw was Fay Grote. The foreman stood not thirty feet away, directly ahead, watching Beaver Crandall and one of the new riders pile brush against the west wall of the already flaming stable. He had his gun in hand. It came up for a fast, snap shot when he saw Dan and Borrasco come out of the building. Dan fired instantly. The charge caught Grote in the chest and hurled him backwards. Instantly the yard became a pandemonium of gunshots and yelling men.

"Watch him!"

At Borrasco's warning, Dan whirled and blasted at Beaver Crandall coming in on his right, gun thundering. Dan missed and, shotgun empty, lunged to one side, breaking the weapon, pulling out the spent shells and reloading all in one motion. He felt a searing pain along his ribs and knew one of Crandall's bullets had creased him. He fired as he moved. Crandall stopped as the load caught him, spun him about and dropped him into the dust.

Replacing the cartridge, Dan started toward the burning main house. The yard was filled with a haze of smoke and the odor of gunpowder, and somewhere a horse was screaming in mortal agony. Humboldt and Dunaway were trying to climb into their saddles, but their mounts, frightened out of their wits by the confusion, kept shying away. A third man was already aboard and racing for the gate, having had his fill. Dan could see Lilith and the new man, Buster Clagg. Clagg was trying to draw her around the corner of the house, out of the line of stray bullets. Over on his right Gordon Sharp was hobbling toward them, shooting as he came; he was having difficulty with his bad leg, and his bullets were doing little damage.

Dan fired at the escaping rider, saw him wince in the saddle and then, bending lower, drive spurs into his horse. He was quickly out of range. Dunaway and Humboldt were on their horses and coming in fast, guns setting up a steady rattle. Dan dodged to one side and fired at the nearest — Humboldt. The rider was jarred by the shock but came on, his pistol still barking. Dan felt the breath of another bullet, this time along his neck.

"Here's one for your friend Dunaway!" John Borrasco called from the side.

Ruick was aware of two rapid blasts. He saw Nathan Dunaway stiffen in the stirrups, almost standing upright, and then topple heavily. In the same moment Bill Humboldt's bay horse, riderless, came trotting back across the yard.

"That ought to finish it," Ruick said grimly to Borrasco.

There was no answer, and he turned.

The bounty hunter was down on his knees. He had a surprised, wondering look on his face, and his thin lips were twisted into a rueful grin. With both hands pressed to his breast he stared at Ruick.

"Damn — if I don't — think they — got me," he gasped, and fell forward.

The yard was suddenly hushed. Dan glanced about. Gordon Sharp was sitting on the ground, apparently unhurt but a victim of his own disability. Humboldt's pony was standing near that of Dunaway's, and the injured one that had been screaming had ceased its cries.

"That's all of 'em!" Sharp shouted.

Dan dropped to his knees beside Borrasco, took him gently by the shoulders, and turned him over. He was dead. The long trail had ended nowhere for him, after all. He got slowly to his feet, the presence of death all around the yard filling him with a depressive sickness. Why must a gun always be the answer to every question, to every argument?

The others were coming up — Lilith and Clagg from the far side of the main house, Heggem and Joe Harley from points along the yard.

"It's over with!" Heggem yelled before he was close. "We've finished Dunaway once and for all. I sure take back all I said and thought about you, Ruick. Hadn't been for you and your friend here, we'd have lost everything."

Dan ignored the rancher. He turned to Lilith. "You all right?"

She gave him a faint smile. "I'm all right. Did you — are you? Standing out there with all that shooting — I —"

"Couple of close ones. No more than that," he answered.

"My sentiments about you exactly," Gordon Sharp took up where Heggem had left off. "Always knew there was good stuff in you, Dan. All it needed was bringin' out!"

Dan favored the old rancher with a wry grin. "Leo the only one to get hurt?"

Clagg nodded soberly. "He's dead. But the only one. It's a tough thing, but I reckon we were lucky at that. We owe you a lot, Ruick."

"You don't owe me but one thing," Dan replied in a weary voice. "The man who killed my brother. Who is he?"

There was an immediate silence. Gordon Sharp cleared his throat. Heggem began to fill his pipe from a doeskin tobacco pouch.

"That was the bargain," Dan reminded them coldly. "I held up my end, now you hold up yours."

Lilith McCall stepped up to him. She looked into his eyes, her face calm and sad. "I'm the one you want, Dan. I shot your brother."

25

Lilith's words were like a whip slashing across Dan Ruick's face. He stared at her unbelievingly — it wasn't so, it could not be. His glance lifted to Heggem, to Sharp. Both men turned away.

Lilith stood very stiff and straight. Sunlight glistened brightly on her wealth of dark hair and pointed up the contour of her face, the blue of her eyes.

"How —" he began, and halted, helpless.

"I didn't mean for it to be him," she said then. "I'm not trying to worm out of it. It was a bullet from my rifle, fired by me, that killed him. But it was an accident."

"Accident? How can shooting a man from ambush be an accident?" There was no anger in Dan's tone, only wonder.

"My husband and I had been hunting strays. We didn't own many, so we missed them soon after they drifted off. We found them, about a dozen steers in a small canyon, and were driving them back.

"We heard horses and saw Grote and several others, including your brother, coming. My husband insisted that I go on ahead in case there was trouble. He was always afraid of Grote where I was concerned. He stayed with the cattle, and I rode on toward the ranch. I heard shooting soon after I left and went back to where I could see what was happening. Grote was sitting with the others, all of them still in the saddle, deliberately trying to shoot my husband. It was only that he was having a bad time with the cattle, and kept riding back and forth, that saved him.

"I had my rifle. I took it out and aimed it at Grote. I fired but missed him, and the bullet hit your brother, who was just beyond. It was my poor shooting that did it."

An accident. Somehow Dan felt a load lift from his shoulders, from his heart. Not that it lessened the death of Albert to any degree — he was still the victim of a bullet. But somehow it was different.

"I'm ready," Lilith's voice broke through his thoughts. "Let me get my horse and I'll ride into town with you." She started across the yard, heading for the corral, where the horses had gathered from the flames.

Dan said, "No need for that. This thing ended here, today."

Gordon Sharp heaved a relieved sigh and, hobbling up, clapped him on the shoulder. "Fine. Fine! Like I just said, I knew you was made of the right stuff!"

Dan gave him a close glance. The old rancher had not always felt that way, not by a lot. But that, too, belonged to the past now.

Lilith's shoulders had slumped, now the strain of the past hours was over. She turned her back on the men and, woman-like, began to weep softly, the shock and horror at last breaking down her reserve. John Heggem moved to her side and placed his arm about her.

"It's all right, girl," he said in an awkward, kind way. "Everything's all right now."

"You bet it is!" Gordon Sharp said cheerfully. "We'll all pitch in and rebuild this place of yours in jig time! And then mine. We'll get all the ranchers around here to lend a hand. By George, they owe us plenty, us keepin' Dunaway off their necks! And we'll get you started on that place of yours, Dan. Loan you enough stock to get goin'."

"Sure," Heggem added. "Won't take long. And we better commence on these buildings right soon. Won't be long till cold weather. For a starter, Dan, just happened to think I've got about fifty head that'll make good breeding stock. I'll have the boys trot 'em down your way tomorrow."

"And you can figure on more," Joe Harley said. "Folks around here ain't soon going to forget what you did this day for them. They'll be grateful, and they'll show it."

Dan Ruick felt a new, unfamiliar warmness filter through his body; these people were *being* his friends, wanting to help him, asking him to become a part of their life. It was a new experience. He glanced from one to the other, uncertain. It was the sort of life he had forever dreamed of, hoped for, but never expected to attain. And there was Lilith, smiling expectantly at him, hoping his decision would be the right one. Someday, perhaps when her grief was lost in the shadows of the past and Albert was no longer in his own mind, perhaps then they could become better acquainted — possibly find a new life together. He could visualize nothing greater, more complete than having Lilith as his wife and a fine little spread of their own to live on. And it wouldn't take much to rebuild their ranches. With the help of the others, it could soon be accomplished.

But it could not be.

He realized that in the next moment. Involuntarily he glanced over his shoulder to the still body of John Borrasco — the symbol of his past. There could be no future with Lilith so long as there was the past with its unsatisfied demands. John Borrasco was dead, yes; but there were other John Borrascos who would take up the chase. Nothing ended with the bounty man's death except his own life. Dan knew he could ride on, forget Lilith and the Silver Flats and again be forever on the drift until one day, when he would make a mistake or was not fast enough with his gun.

Or he could stay now, accept the offer of Gordon Sharp and the other ranchers — and some day have to stand and face the inevitable accounting, breaking Lilith's heart in the process. Or he could ride back, face his accusers now — get it over with, have done with it one way or another.

For a long minute he stared at the irregular skyline of the Angosturas. It was a fine land, one hard to leave; but a man who could not possess the things he loved with a clear conscience and in peace possessed nothing in reality.

"One thing more, boy." Gordon Sharp's voice was a sober sound. "I'll be straightenin' out some of this feelin' about your pa. I ain't proud I was one of that mob the day it happened, and I been sorry, real down deep, for what took place, because there wasn't no real proof. I reckon I just wasn't man enough to own up to it. And maybe too ashamed. But I'll fix that mighty quick. You can depend on it."

Dan nodded to the old rancher. He supposed he should feel some anger for the injustice done his father and the rest of the Ruicks but somehow it no longer mattered. He turned to face Lilith.

"I'm obliged to you all," he said slowly, "but I can't be taking up your offer — not right at this time. It isn't that I don't want to and don't appreciate it. It's been my dream to have a spread of my own, and I'd about decided it was something that wasn't going to be."

"Then why not —" Heggem began and stopped.

"Few things I've got to do, straighten out, you might call it. Reckon it'll keep me away for a spell."

Lilith gave him a quick smile, her eyes suddenly bright with tears. He knew his decision had been her hope.

"But I'll be back. Soon."

"I know," she said. "I'll pray — and be waiting for you."

"Couldn't ask for anything more," Dan Ruick said, and, wheeling, he started for his roan horse.

We hope you have enjoyed this Large Print book. Other Thorndike, Wheeler or Chivers Press Large Print books are available at your library or directly from the publishers.

For more information about current and up-coming titles, please call or write, without ob-ligation, to:

Publisher
Thorndike Press
295 Kennedy Memorial Drive
Waterville, ME   04901
Tel. (800) 223-1244

Or visit our Web site at:
www.gale.com/thorndike
www.gale.com/wheeler

OR

Chivers Large Print
published by BBC Audiobooks Ltd
St James House, The Square
Lower Bristol Road
Bath BA2 3SB
England
Tel. +44(0) 800 136919
email: bbcaudiobooks@bbc.co.uk
www.bbcaudiobooks.co.uk

All our Large Print titles are designed for easy reading, and all our books are made to last.